GLASS AND STONE

What Reviewers Say About
Renee Roman's Work

Where the Lies Hide

"I like the concept of the novel. The story idea is well thought out and well researched. I really connected with Cam's character..."
—*Rainbow Reflections*

"[T]his book is just what I needed. There's plenty of romantic tension, intrigue, and mystery. I wanted Sarah to find her brother as much as she did, and I struggled right alongside Cam in her discoveries."—*Kissing Backwards*

"Overall, a really great novel. Well written incredible characters, an interesting investigation storyline and the perfect amount of sexy times."—*Books, Life and Everything Nice*

"This is a fire and ice romance wrapped up in an engaging crime plot that will keep you hooked."—*Istoria Lit*

Epicurean Delights

"[*Epicurean Delights*] is captivating, with delightful humor and well-placed banter taking place between the two characters. ...[T]he main characters are lovable and easily become friends we'd like to see succeed in life and in love."—*Lambda Literary Review*

"Hard Body"

"[T]he tenderness and heat make it a great read."—*reviewer @large*

"[A] short erotic story that has some beautiful emotional moments."—*Kitty Kat's Book Review Blog*

By the Author

Epicurean Delights

Stroke of Fate

Hard Body

Where the Lies Hide

Bonded Love

Body Language

Hot Days, Heated Nights

Escorted

Glass and Stone

GLASS AND STONE

by

Renee Roman

2022

GLASS AND STONE
© 2022 By Renee Roman. All Rights Reserved.

ISBN 13: 978-1-63679-162-3

This Trade Paperback Original Is Published By
Bold Strokes Books, Inc.
P.O. Box 249
Valley Falls, NY 12185

First Edition: October 2022

Credits
Editors: Victoria Villaseñor and Cindy Cresap
Production Design: Susan Ramundo
Cover Design By Tammy Seidick

Acknowledgments

To the family I was fortunate enough to be welcomed into, I will forever be grateful to Radclyffe and Bold Strokes Books.

And to the readers who continue to support writers everywhere, especially this one, thank you for your loyalty.

Dedication

This book is dedicated to those
who have lost loved ones to suicide.
May the memories that bring you joy
outweigh those of your sorrow.

CHAPTER ONE

The air around her swirled with fine particles as saws buzzed and drills whirred. Jordan Spade stood with her hands on her hips and surveyed her current jobsite. It was something she made herself do every now and then as a way of staying in the here and now. Life was good. Even when her misery hung over her like a storm cloud about to let loose on her, she'd learned to step through it, push on, be strong.

"Hey, boss." Gary, the drywall contractor, called to her from the makeshift driveway.

"Morning. What's up?" She reached into her back pocket for the small notebook with ragged edges and produced a pen from another. When a tradesman talked there was information to be had.

"There's a delay in Sheetrock. It's going to set us behind a few days."

Jordan shook her head. The pandemic had impacted every business and every household in one way or another, and the housing industry had suffered right along with everyone else. Building construction was moving forward in fits and starts as materials came in at a crawl. Setbacks were the norm these days and everyone she spoke to was looking forward to a better sense of normalcy.

"Okay, Gary. Let me know when it comes in so I can get the other trades up to snuff." She marked it in her book then shoved it away as she calculated the timetable impact. Painters, window and door installers, and a few others would have to be put on hold. They'd move on to another job in the meantime, and sometimes the result was another delay for her while they finished up at another location.

"Sure thing. I'm going to tell my guys to clean up and head out for the day. We've got another job a few blocks over so as soon as the materials are delivered, we'll come back."

Gary was a good guy. Dependable and fair. Her crews were top-notch too, even if one or two of the guys were total jerks, the quality of their work made the annoying instances tolerable. After finishing her inspection, she pulled the blueprints from her truck and spread them across the tailgate, her clipboard nearby. She systematically checked off completed items and jotted necessary changes.

There were several small notations she hadn't paid previous attention to, but they were in tiny print and barely readable. Jordan grumbled. From her glove box she produced a magnifying glass and zeroed in on the areas. *Stained-glass inset.* It was odd that she had no recollection of this when she'd gone over the first set of prints, though it wasn't unusual for owners to change their mind during construction, often adding and subtracting things as the full picture came to fruition or they saw a TV show and now wanted to include some obscure detail in their own build. As she flipped through the oversized pages she focused on similar notes, and she made a new entry. *Stained-glass windows.*

Obviously, these were going to be done once her crew was gone, so she didn't have to think about it. Just the same, she'd contact the owners. Sometimes changes were made after the prints were completed and the builder didn't have them reprinted. It made for a lot of frustration, and she didn't need any more of that in her life.

❖

Colors burst against the wall, a kaleidoscope of blues, greens, and purples. Callie Burke smiled at the piece that perfectly matched the vision she had when her customer had given her the color palette and a bit of information about her friend's likes, based on the album she was shown. It would be a beautiful birthday present and she wrapped the stained-glass suncatcher in bubble wrap then placed it gently in the box. A few minutes later, she'd finished it with a delicate linen paper and a purple bow.

Display pieces of different shapes and sizes hung in the windows and along the wall. Unlike canvas, it would take centuries for the sun to fade the colors in the glass, and she loved the permanency of her art. The coffee maker beeped, and she put a splash of cream and a little sugar in her cup before adding the brew. The aroma reminded her of that trip to Cape Cod and the bistro on Commercial Street that made the *best* coffee she'd ever tasted. Once a month, a pound would be delivered right to her door. The first sip was heaven, just like each day she made it, and she enjoyed a few minutes of the peace that she'd come to love before getting back to work. If it was quiet and she really listened, she could hear the ocean in the distance since her home was only a couple of blocks from the shore.

Callie opened her sketchbook and reviewed the email confirmation from a homeowner who'd asked for some commission work. Her mentor had often let her imagination take over when there was a request for a custom piece. That experience had given her the confidence to take an order for a home in her parents' neighborhood and reinforced the idea that she could make it on her own.

Since moving to the area, she'd been lucky to be contacted for some work in a home that was being built for a friend of a friend. It included a window between the bathroom and hallway, and custom replacement panes for the front door. A Tiffany-like lampshade for the small workstation in the kitchen. Four globes for over the massive island. With the dimensions stated, in theory she could begin working, except she knew better. It was time she visited the house under construction to take her own measurements. The inserts had to be within an eighth of an inch on all sides and perfectly square, otherwise the glass wouldn't sit correctly, and the small gaps would allow for expansion of the wood in damp weather. There was little room for error, and she didn't want to waste expensive pieces of glass because she was too lazy to do the leg work. Tomorrow would be the day to make sure everything was as it should be.

Callie refilled her mug before entering the modest spare room that would eventually hold a guest bed, nightstands, and chest of drawers. There wasn't any doubt her mother would be quizzing her endlessly about when they could come for a visit from the hell-hole heat of Florida. Her parents vowed to never leave and at one time she'd felt the same way, but her teenage infatuation with being a beach bunny faded once she'd been through several hurricane seasons. The fear of losing her home and everything that was near and dear to her was real, though she'd decided to stick it out until after college. Her master's degree hung in a frame in the hallway, but she hoped it was a showpiece more than a representation of her profession.

Callie picked up her sketchbook and coffee, then headed into the makeshift workspace. When it wasn't too hot, she worked in the garage and opened the big door, spreading materials out on the temporary table she'd set up. When it was beastly, she worked in the air-conditioned house. Today was one of those days.

Until she found someone reasonable and reliable to work on the garage and turn it into a split space workroom and showroom for her beloved art, she was making do. Besides, there wasn't any rush to heft all her totes again, but when the time came she'd manage. She'd have to rely on herself from now on. She had yet to make friends and hadn't dated in months. A girlfriend would complicate things and distract her from turning her art into a way of making a living. Not that she'd ever had a girlfriend, at least none that qualified as one. As a teenager who'd fumbled around with her sexuality, she'd been a loner and preferred it that way. Uncomplicated. But she couldn't help thinking about a nice, casual sexual encounter. One that wouldn't interfere with her plans. With a sigh, she pushed that thought away. Failing to focus could mean failure, and she wasn't about to let that happen.

CHAPTER TWO

The GPS was fickle today and Callie circled the neighbor-hood a couple of times before finding the home she was looking for that was likely in mid-construction. She was pleasantly surprised to find the outside nearly complete except for landscaping and some trim. She grabbed her tote bag from the front seat and tossed her keys in the side pocket. It was easy to tell the sprawling home demanded special touches to help make it interesting, not just beautiful. As she got closer, sounds of workers greeted her, and she walked through the open garage in search of whoever was in charge.

Though construction materials were scattered throughout, it wasn't hard to locate the kitchen that occupied a huge amount of space in the center of the home. The countertops were missing, but the cabinet measurements were drawn on the walls and the floor was outlined with tape as placeholders, so she set her bag down, and pulled out a tape measure and clipboard, forgetting she should tell someone she was there. Above where she stood were four evenly spaced electrical boxes and Callie began to measure the distance between them. She'd just started when a gruff voice broke her concentration.

"Who the hell are you?"

Callie glanced up and smiled. "Oh, hi. I'm Callie Burke. Do you know who's in charge?" The stern expression that met hers should have given her an indication her presence wasn't welcome, but her indomitable spirit refused to be intimidated. The woman took a few steps closer, holding a clipboard similar to the one she had just set down, and banged it against her thigh in annoyance.

"I'm the general contractor, Jordan Spade." Jordan's eyes were honey brown, her face and arms deeply tanned, her lips pulled into a line. She was handsome, Callie had to give her that even if she was being a tad rude.

"Great. I was going to look for you, but I got sidetracked." She waved to the space that was outlined with masking tape and likely where the island would be located, then moved forward with her hand extended. "It's nice to meet you." Jordan's hand closed over hers, the texture rough and emanating warmth.

"What are you doing here?" Jordan's aggravation seemed to be escalating.

"Sorry. I'm the stained-glass artist the homeowners contracted to make pendant lamp shades and some window inserts." She cocked her head. "Didn't they tell you?"

Jordan blew out a breath. "No. There was a vague mention on the blueprints, but..." She shook her head. "Doesn't matter. So what are you doing in here?"

"Taking distance measurements. I didn't think I'd be bothering anyone since there's no one working in here." She reached in her bag and produced a business card, using it to keep her from feeling out of sorts.

Jordan gave the card a quick glance and tucked it under the clamp on her worn clipboard. "The floor tiles are going to be installed next week. You won't be able to walk in here for a few days."

"That's fine. I won't have the shades ready for a few weeks. It takes time to create art. But the other windows—"

"Others?" Jordan pulled her hand down her face.

She picked up her clipboard and ran down the list. "I'm confident I can get it all done in a month or so." Just then a loud bang echoed through the home.

"Son of a bitch." Jordan looked at her. "I'll be right back."

Callie watched her go. Her stride full of purpose, her thick thighs straining her jeans and the veins in her arms prominent. Jordan's overall demeanor had been less than friendly and from the sound of what just happened, she was fairly certain it wasn't going to improve. In the meantime, she had work to do. A few minutes later, she heard a deep rumbling voice approaching.

"If one more freaking thing goes..." Jordan stopped mumbling when she realized Callie was still there.

She jotted down a number and looked up. "Everything okay?"

Jordan's bark was sharp. "Is it ever?"

She wanted to tell Jordan to stick it where the sun doesn't shine, but instead she smiled kindly. Being in her position couldn't be easy. "That depends on if there's a lot of moving parts."

Jordan's laugh sounded lighter. "Isn't that the truth. What else do you need here?"

Callie went back to her list. "The master bath, the hall foyer, and the front door."

"Kind of all over the place then."

"If this is a bad time, I can..."

"It's not gonna get any better, Ms. Burke." Jordan rapped her knuckles on the door casing. "Sometimes it actually gets worse. Come on, I'll show you where the rooms are and then I've got to get going."

"Sure. That's fine." She gathered her stuff and followed Jordan through a maze of framed walls, some with Sheetrock, and some that had little at all done. They stepped into a large rectangular room with plumbing for a double sink and what would be, if she was interpreting the layout correctly, a huge walk-in shower. The area above where the toilet would be had an approximately twenty-four-inch opening that was covered with plastic. "I need an exact measurement. Can I remove the plastic?"

Jordan nodded, then she carefully peeled back the masking tape and held the plastic out of the way.

She measured twice. "Wow. That rarely happens."

"What does?" Jordan leaned against the wall, looking between the opening and her clipboard.

"It's exactly square." She finished a note on the paper, glanced up, and winked. "Makes my life a lot easier."

"I'll be sure to pass your approval on to the workers."

Callie couldn't tell if Jordan was kidding or not. "Thanks. I won't be much longer." Jordan looked like she was about to say something but stopped. Instead she replaced the plastic then pulled a bent business card from her back pocket and handed it to her.

"Call me when you're ready to install and I'll let you know a day when there aren't a million things going on." After showing her the other areas, Jordan returned them to the kitchen. "Can you find your way out when you're done?"

"Yes, I'll be fine. Thanks, Jordan."

Jordan gave a nod and a tight smile, then disappeared. As far as first impressions went, Jordan's didn't give her the warm fuzzies, but then she had just waltzed in on her jobsite unannounced. Maybe the next time she saw her would be less awkward for them both. She could hope anyway.

CHAPTER THREE

Jordan rubbed the side of her head to ward off the impending headache. The day had started out pretty calm before the interloper had shown up. After that, things seemed to steamroll downhill.

The bang that had startled both of them had been made by the lift dropping a skid of shingles onto the roof. The operator had blamed the gears seizing, but that would have only been believable if the lift had stopped working. More than likely, it was operator error. She'd gone to look at the trusses and discovered a small crack that would only get bigger over time. After swearing in Technicolor, she contacted her roofer foreman and he assured her they could replace the damaged piece without a lot of lost time, though the added expense would have to come out of the contingency budget. So much for planning ahead.

She twirled the bottle of beer that was tepid and still half full. As rare as it was, she wasn't in the mood to drink. Jordan didn't really know what she was in the mood for. Maybe she was tired. Weeks had skittered by without a good night's sleep. Flashes of the past, mingling with the present, kept her awake, though she rarely saw anything of the future. Did that mean she didn't have one as far as new things, new experiences went? Nothing different than the bleak past that followed her into the present? God, that was a sobering thought. As unimaginable as the future might be for her, she had hoped for a few uplifting moments.

Ignoring deep thinking had been Jordan's wheelhouse for too long. A few years ago, her entire world had been flipped off its axis. The tragic loss left her numb and unable to function. Not only had her father died by his own hand, but because she'd been so into herself she hadn't been around much. Maybe if she had been…no. The promise she made to stop blaming herself was an ongoing battle. It didn't help that the business pulled her in so many directions she hadn't talked with Mel in more than a week. Another promise broken. The sigh that came from her toes channeled through her, churning as it went.

She pushed the beer aside and signaled the bartender. "Can I get a burger and fries?"

"Sure thing, Jor." He yelled the order through a window. "What are you drinking?"

"Coffee." The caffeine would also churn unpleasantly in her stomach, but it was a better alternative than the whiskey she wanted. Once she started, there would be a lot more than one, and she'd pay for it tomorrow. Sex would be a good way to take her mind off the job and what dark thoughts lurked inside her brain, but that would be another mistake. No woman would want her in her current state of unrest and unease. Whoever it might be, they deserved better.

Mike slid the plate in front of her and took her money. There was lettuce sticking out from the roll and she focused on it. What had drawn her to notice how vivid green it was? *Callie.* Callie's eyes were that green, like fresh grass. She'd been captivated at the first glance and the undauntable smile. Then her survival defenses had kicked in. Jordan had to make a conscious decision to not react hastily, and she wasn't sure she succeeded, but at least she'd found out who she was and what the hell she was doing in the house. The "artist" she vaguely remembered hearing about months ago should have jogged some bit of brain matter, but there were bigger things happening not only on that job, but on another. To her semi-warped mind, artist meant Van Gogh or Michelangelo. Like wall murals and such. Finding out stained glass was an art was a big surprise. When Callie handed over her business card, the small nicks and cuts on her finger were visible signs of her profession.

Jordan reached for a fry and came up empty. When had that happened? She looked at her plate to find half of a burger, two pickle slices, and scattered salt. "God, I'm losing it." The bite of burger felt like a lump in her throat. Standing, Jordan pulled a five-dollar bill from her pocket and finished her coffee in a quick slurp.

"Thanks, Mike. See you next time."

The fresh air hit her hard, and she sucked in a lungful. She could leave her truck until morning. It wouldn't be the first time. Mike lived over the bar and the security system kept vandals away. The walk would help clear her jumbled thoughts. Jordan practiced deep breathing while she strode down the uneven sidewalk toward home. Her heartrate slowed and her shoulders relaxed a bit. Now all she had to do was conjure up a picture. Leaning her back against a tree, Jordan closed her eyes, and her mind reached for a pleasant memory but the vision that appeared wasn't what she expected.

Callie stood before her with those amazing green eyes and dark auburn waves of thick-looking hair. The kind she'd gladly run her fingers through. Jordan's eyes opened wide in shock. "What the fuck?" she said out loud, then glanced around. Where the hell had that come from? Sure, Callie was pretty and hadn't been put off by her rather abrupt approach. That still wasn't any reason to be thinking about a stranger when she was supposed to be relaxing. She pushed away from the tree and headed home, alone.

❖

Callie leaned over the sheet of blue glass and pressed the template on top, then traced each pattern piece with a Sharpie. She scored the larger sections and carefully applied even pressure with the running pliers along the score line, listening for the telltale sound of cracking glass. As each piece broke away, she carefully set it aside on the clean work area. The design she'd chosen for the front door wasn't intricate, but the pieces had to be laid out in precise order for the desired effect. The geometric pattern in contrasting colors would draw the eye in and was loosely based on the sketch the homeowner provided.

The other window and art pieces would take a lot more time to complete, but the most important one was this one because it would greet visitors as they arrived at the home. The entrance itself wasn't dramatic, but considering the size of the home it should be. The understated entry was a nod to not everything being as it seemed on the outside. The inside was spacious and a decorator's paradise. Callie used her imagination to picture how it would look finished. She'd have to ask the owners if she could return when it was done.

The clock above her worktable made her groan. It was later than she thought. The rumble of her empty stomach should have provided a clue she'd been there too long. Boxes were still piled along one wall, all neatly labeled and ready whenever she was, if only she could find the time...and the energy. The house had been a great find in a quaint part of town where the front room of the garage of the multi-hued houses often served as boutiques or shops, while the rear was the owner's home. In her case, there was a large double garage that she viewed as a blank canvas. It would cost her a small fortune to convert it to a showroom and workshop, but the end result would be well worth the expense... another aspiration that was now within reach.

She went to the kitchen and opened the refrigerator. Bare-bone contents were all that remained inside. Half-and-half. A partial loaf of bread that was likely moldy by now. Orange juice. A container of unidentifiable, off-color mounds she couldn't remember having which she immediately dumped into the trash.

After removing her apron, she glanced at her clothes. For as late as it was, they'd do. Who would be about at this time of night except for an occasional pedestrian now and then? Nine o'clock on a weeknight meant she wasn't likely to see anyone she knew, not that she'd met many people in her neighborhood yet. Callie grabbed her keys and phone, before making sure all the doors were locked. The area appeared well kept, clean, and safe, but she wasn't leaving anything to chance after sacrificing one dream for another.

The summer night was warm, but the breeze helped keep the air pleasant and Callie swung her arms as she strode along, taking in the sights and sounds she hadn't had a chance to really enjoy since the move. As she neared the small, eclectic main street lined with restaurants, shops, and a few bars, she glanced to her left as she tried to decide which way to head. A figure she vaguely recognized had stopped a half block away, then leaned against a mature tree. The move was rather odd. The person hadn't been weaving like someone who'd had a few too many drinks, but she considered going to see if they needed help anyway. After a moment, the figure righted and kept going. Obviously not in need of assistance, she turned right, and Callie shrugged. There was a bar a few buildings away that one of the movers she'd hired to empty the storage container had recommended for a decent late-night burger. Comfort food wasn't something she indulged in often, but when she did she went all in. Tonight was an "all in" kind of night and would give her a chance to review how much fun completing the pieces for the house would be, despite the ornery temperament of the woman in charge.

❖

"Just stick to the specs and don't go rogue on me, all right?"

The carpenter nodded. "You got it, Jordan."

She swept her arm across her brow and moved to the next room. The flooring in the guest bathroom would be done soon and she wanted the base cabinet in after that. She hated when people cut corners by installing the flooring around cabinets rather than running it all the way to the walls. That mentality forced any future renovations to include new flooring, whether it was necessary or not. The back-ordered Sheetrock had been hung and all the rooms were primed, but the final coats of color were going to have to wait until the paint arrived next week. Another delay, and that meant more money bleeding from the contingency budget. As she entered the master bathroom, she stopped short. The framed-out window between the bedroom and bath, where Callie had measured for her glass inset, had been covered with sheet rock.

"Son of a bitch," Jordan hissed under her breath. She turned the corner and stormed off to find the drywall guys. They were sitting around outside of the garage shooting the shit and having lunch. "Who blocked the opening in the master bath?" There wasn't a good reason to not make her displeasure apparent, so she went with it.

"I did. What's the problem?" one of the younger guys piped up.

"The problem," she said, "is the opening was for a commissioned piece of stained glass." She held the blueprints up. "Did you even check why it had been left that way?"

"Actually, I did, but I guess I missed that detail, so I covered it."

Jordan clenched her ever-present clipboard tighter. "When you finish lunch, take it out and make sure you don't change the original dimensions." The last thing she needed was for Callie to find out what had happened and ream her a new one. Callie had sent a text saying she had a piece done and wanted to install it, and Jordan hoped the error was corrected before she showed. As if summoned by some sort of ironic magic, Callie pulled up to the curb. She slid a long box from the back and smiled as she carried it up the walkway. Jordan met her in front of the garage.

"Hi. What have you got there?" she asked.

"It's the insert for the front door." Callie gestured to the bubble-wrapped contents. "And I want to remeasure the other places to make sure they're still correct for the rest of the pieces."

Looking up, Jordan pulled from her negotiation strategies. "So about that, are you sure you need to remeasure? I thought you got everything you needed the first time." She tried to sound less unsure than she felt.

"I know, but once it's done, there's no going back so I want to be sure." Callie tipped her head. "Is getting into the rooms going to be a problem?"

Jordan's jaw clenched. "No. There's an issue with the master bath though."

Callie's brows knit. "If I can't get in there today, I'll come back tomorrow. This will take me at least an hour to install, so it's not a wasted trip."

"The window opening was covered with Sheetrock." She heard the snickers behind her. "I'll have it removed as soon as possible."

Callie set the box gently down. "What happened? You knew there was glass going in there, right?"

Ignoring the audience, Jordan forged ahead. "Yes. You were quite clear about what you were installing, but the Sheetrock crew didn't check with anyone and boarded over the bedroom side. It'll be fixed today."

Callie's right foot tapped the ground and her lips pulled into a thin line. "Okay, well, like I said, I can come back. I'll work on the front door and come back in a couple of days."

She could tell from her stiff posture as she turned away that Callie wasn't happy, but there wasn't much she could do at the moment. She'd pissed off enough women in her time to know she had one more to add to the list. Jordan went inside while Callie went to her car. A few minutes later she heard a strident noise and loud laughter. Then Callie's distinctive voice. She strode swiftly to the garage and pulled up short at the scene before her.

Jordan watched as a few of the workers whistled and hooted like wolves while Callie was bent over moving objects near the front entrance. Her backside was on full display under tight jean shorts. Thankfully, they weren't super short or else everyone would have had an eyeful. She flicked her gaze just as one man jabbed the other before eliciting a catcall. When he proceeded to tell Callie how hot she was, Jordan had heard enough.

"What the hell is going on," Jordan said. Her tone was more of a roar than a question, and it made Callie jump. "Is this how you speak to the women in your lives?" She glanced at Callie, and she wasn't sure if she was grateful or pissed. Callie stood with her hands on her hips.

"Too bad I don't bat for your team, fellas. And I certainly wouldn't put out for anyone who doesn't even know the difference between a blueprint cutout and a mistake." Callie turned away.

The last remark reduced the crew to low grumbles, and Jordan felt compelled to do more. "Lunch is over. I'm not paying you to stand around." Sufficiently chagrined, at least for the time being, they went inside.

When she made eye contact with Callie, Jordan was confused by what she saw. Frustration, or disappointment, or embarrassment. Disappointment wasn't new to her, but she had to make sure Callie knew she wasn't going to ignore the issue. "I'll make sure that doesn't happen again. Sorry."

"Don't make a big deal out of it. No harm, no foul. It's not the first time I've dealt with their kind." Callie waved her hand in dismissal.

Jordan didn't have a clue why Callie wasn't angry at how she'd been treated, but her red face suggested otherwise. Obviously, she was mad. What else could it have been? The lightbulb went on. Callie was embarrassed. "I was trying to help. I didn't mean to embarrass you."

"Mmm...thanks." Callie didn't look up from what she was doing. "I can look out for myself."

There was nothing left to say. She'd stepped in to help, but it backfired. Did Callie think she did it just to showboat rather than caring that Callie receive the respect she deserved? Even as her gut twisted, she knew it was better to let Callie be than to push. She didn't really know her. All she knew about Callie was that she was intelligent and beautiful...and was much too good for the likes of Jordan.

CHAPTER FOUR

Callie didn't need anyone to come to her defense, but that it had been Jordan made the situation that much more of an embarrassment. She didn't want someone she'd had words with a few days ago to feel obligated to step in when it wasn't necessary. She was just about to put the guys in their place when Jordan had shown up and made sure the uncouth men knocked it off in no uncertain terms.

At their first meeting, Jordan had been quick to call her out as a virtual trespasser and the ensuing aggravation of showing her around had been quite clear. Then Callie noticed the hint of unease in Jordan's eyes, and she didn't know how to interpret it. There was something else going on other than Jordan controlling her workers, even though she was likely responsible for everything that happened on a site.

Shrugging off the lingering questions, Callie used a small screwdriver to remove the molding holding the frosted glass in place on the entry door. Once it was off, she carefully scored the caulk and used a putty knife to remove it. Holding the edge of the door between her knees, Callie pushed the glass pane outward, then carefully removed it. The owners told her she could reuse the glass. She never turned down free materials. The opening measurement was one-eighth of an inch larger than her piece. It would be a perfect fit, with room for expansion in warm weather.

After brushing off the edges of the opening to clear away any remaining debris, Callie unwrapped the piece and set it in place. The process would have been easier with another pair of hands. She wasn't about to ask for help from Jordan after saying she could handle things, though. She slid a few glazier points at strategic spots to hold it before fully letting go. The all-weather putty she used would keep rain and snow from getting between the glass and the molding. She scooped out a ball and warmed it in her hands, making it pliable before shaping it into a long rope, then she pressed it against the space where wood and glass met. Once she had all four sides done, she used the putty knife to trim and smooth each strip. With the molding back in place, she removed any putty that had oozed up and gently washed the glass. The whole process had taken less than an hour and the end result made her smile.

Callie piled her tools into the empty box, then slid it into the back of her car. She thought about going inside to find Jordan to let her know she was done, even though it was a bad idea. She strode through the open garage with purpose and stopped when she saw Jordan leaning against a wall, head down and eyes closed. She took a step back, wanting to give her privacy, and something crunched under her foot. Jordan's head jerked up, her eyes expressive and pain filled.

"I didn't mean to disturb you."

"You didn't," Jordan said, though everything about her body posture stated otherwise.

She pointed in the general direction of the front door. "I'm finished, but the putty won't be hard-set until tomorrow, so it should be moved as little as possible." Jordan nodded and continued to look at her, her gaze soulful. Callie wanted to touch her. Give her a bit of comfort she thought she might need, but she couldn't imagine why she'd do such a thing. She shook her head. What a strange thought to have about a woman she barely knew. "Will you call when the bathroom window is ready?"

"Yes." Jordan's voice was rough, as though she had been crying.

"Thanks." She turned to go, sensing her presence wasn't welcome before Jordan's fingertips brushed hers.

"I'm sorry your schedule was interrupted."

Callie turned and their eyes met. For a brief instant she recognized desire until Jordan inhaled sharply and a veil of indifference eclipsed everything else that was written there. "It happens." She wanted to tell Jordan it wasn't a big deal, but she didn't want to interrupt whatever this tentative connection between them was with unnecessary words.

"I'll have it fixed today and dried out by tomorrow. Why don't you plan on coming by in two days for that measurement?"

Two days to mull over everything that had happened today. The space would be good for her to put things into perspective. "Sure. That will work." She wanted to say something meaningful, but Jordan wasn't the type of woman she could picture in her life, so she stayed silent. Not that she was thinking in that direction, of course.

❖

Jordan could only imagine what Callie thought of her overstepping a boundary she'd had no idea existed. Callie had stuck up for herself and ended the rude remarks with as much authority as Jordan had. She still wasn't sure if her lingering guilt had made her rush into action, or if she was ashamed she'd momentarily thought of leaving Callie to handle it. In the end it had still been an awkward situation and she wasn't sure exactly what had happened. All she knew was she'd had the guts to speak up for a change. The lack of inertia was a relief. Maybe she wasn't as much of a failure as she thought.

After leaving Callie to work on the door, she'd gone through the house again, checking and rechecking the work yet to be done and the places marked for Callie's glass. She made sure they were highlighted on the blueprints, not wanting any more mistakes when it came to the fit of the special pieces. Bad enough Callie probably thought she was incompetent by hiring sexist morons. The last thing she needed was to have to tell her another mistake had been made.

Once she made a full circle of the interior, Jordan leaned against a wall and closed her eyes. Disappointment wasn't new to her, but it had been a long time since there'd been anyone she cared about enough to worry.

Her father had been her champion, always sticking up for her and wondering what he could do to help make Jordan recognize her worth even while questioning his own ability to instill confidence in her. She hadn't realized how much he wanted her to have faith in her abilities until he was gone. Jordan's heart seized. It was times like these she missed him more than she already did. For the millionth time since his death, she questioned how she could have missed the signs. How she'd been so lost in the turmoil of her own life she'd given little thought to anyone else's. Part of her had blamed her mother for spending every day with him and not seeing something was wrong. It was the main reason they rarely talked.

At first, her coping mechanism had been to not allow room for any kind of relationship in her life. Her chest eased a bit. Mel, her best friend and confidant since high school, was the exception to the rule. Otherwise, Jordan made sure people didn't *want* to get close, letting them only see the hard exterior and gruff persona that shielded her, and others, from having to deal with the eventual fallout of being let down. But as time went on and she grew older, alone forever was losing its appeal. A nearby noise brought her back from the place she often avoided.

Then there was Callie. So beautiful she could cry if she let the emotions take her there. She'd apologized for disturbing her, but Jordan was already disturbed. Had been for a while now. After Callie left with a promise to come back in two days, Jordan had laughed bitterly to herself. Who was she kidding? The flare of desire snuck in at the most inopportune time and she hoped Callie hadn't noticed. Nothing indicated she had, which was good. Jordan wouldn't make promises she couldn't keep, and keeping promises wasn't what she excelled at. Running her business was her forte. The one thing she could be proud of. Being able to complete a job and knowing she'd done her best meant not all was lost.

Whatever hope she'd had for a life of love and happiness had disappeared after the familiar misery had taken hold. She was doing okay without the love and companionship of a woman. One day at a time and moving through life with that mindset was for the best. At least, it was a good argument in her own head.

CHAPTER FIVE

The sound of a saw greeted her as Callie slung her bag over her shoulder and strode to the front door. A quick inspection was followed by a nod of satisfaction. The putty was hard, the seams tight and the window didn't move when she pressed her fingers to the glass and moved them upward. The door wasn't locked, and she pushed it open slowly before stepping onto the dark wood flooring.

"Jordan?" Callie called into the house. A huge pickup truck with *JS, General Contractor*, emblazoned on the side sat at the end of the driveway, so she knew Jordan was there. She was about to call out again when a raspy voice came from behind her, making her jump.

"Looking for me?"

As she spun Callie caught the tail end of a smile Jordan was trying to hide. "Are you following me?" She wanted to laugh until Jordan's teasing gaze turned to panic.

"No…I—" Jordan stammered.

She reached for her and touched her bare forearm, the muscle beneath her fingers twitching. "I'm kidding. I wanted to check with you before going any farther. I didn't know if it was safe to walk on the floors." She let her hand slide away when Jordan's eyes flicked to the point of contact.

"Thanks, but they're all done except for the guest bedroom. Materials are coming in piecemeal, and the subcontractors are working other jobs in between. At this rate, I'll be late for the deadline and over budget." Jordan looked none too happy.

"Certainly you can't be blamed for material delays."

"You'd be surprised what I'm blamed for," Jordan mumbled under her breath, but she caught the words. "You're all set to do your measurements. Let me know if you need anything." Jordan's gaze trailed her body, leaving an unaccustomed warmth, and then she was gone before Callie had time to register her exit.

She moved from room to room and checked the new measurements against her original ones. The opening that had been blocked was slightly smaller than before, but at least it was still square, and the change was minimal. She could live with that. With no reason to hang around, Callie wanted to let Jordan know she was finished. It would be another week before the pendant shades were done, but she wanted to be sure the fixtures over the island would be in place by then.

A painter with a long extension roller worked at the far end of the master bedroom, the wall in front of him partially covered in a rich gray. "Hi," she said. "Have you seen Jordan?"

Following a dip in the paint and a roll on the tray, the man looked up and smiled. "Afternoon, ma'am. Jordan might be out back. She grumbled something about the patio being 'a far cry from perfect' and headed that way."

Callie inwardly smiled. It sounded like she wasn't the only recipient of Jordan's displeasure, although this morning she'd actually verged on being cordial. She walked through the house, mindful of the new finishes and fresh paint, based on the lingering smell. At the far side of the kitchen was a newly installed slider with the molding still missing, and she glanced through it. Jordan sat on a knee-high retaining wall, the leaf-filtered shade making a pattern on her tanned skin. She pulled out a crumpled pack of cigarettes, pulled one out, then fished a lighter from her front pocket.

Satisfied Jordan would stay put for another few minutes, Callie quickly made her way to the car, grabbed the small cooler from the footwell, and hurried back to the slider. When she stepped outside Jordan glanced up, both surprise and pleasure in her expression.

"Please tell me they didn't totally fuck up the cut-out."

She strolled toward the wall and said, "You'll be happy to hear it's fine." She sat down an arm's length away before setting the cooler between them. Jordan appeared suspicious as she lifted a paper coffee cup to her lips.

"Is that from this morning?" Callie tipped her chin in question.

"Cold and barely tolerable seems to be how I finish most of them," Jordan said, then set the empty cup at her feet.

She smiled and opened the cooler to pull out a bowl of fruit, a couple bottles of iced tea, and a thick sandwich. She handed a bottle to Jordan. "This is supposed to be good." Jordan's response, a crooked smile, encouraged her to keep going. "The fruit is from a little stand on a back road I found by accident." Callie produced two plastic forks. She opened the Ziploc, plucked half a sandwich out, placed it on a napkin along with a fork and handed them off to Jordan. "Ham, turkey, and Swiss with mayo." Jordan stared at her. "What?"

"First, thank you. Second, did I miss the lunch invitation somewhere? Third, do you always pack a lunch to be shared?"

Her face heated as she admitted she *had* thought about Jordan while preparing the food, though her original idea had been to find a park to have it in. "You don't have to eat it. I just saw you out here and thought..." She picked at the edge of a lettuce leaf from her half, unable to look at Jordan.

"Thank you, Callie. It's been ages since I've had a homemade lunch." Jordan cracked the seal on the bottle, took a long pull, then nodded. "So, what's next for you," she asked before taking a bite.

"The pendant shades. They'll take the longest to craft, but I'll need to measure fixtures once they're up to be sure the owner hasn't changed them since we spoke."

Jordan seemed thoughtful as she chewed, then swallowed. "This is really good." She took another drink. "Then what? Another house?"

Callie plucked a grape from the container. "Houses are a rare treat. I'll keep working on pieces to display in my shop. Maybe I'll do a few festivals or art shows before the weather turns."

"You live in the city?"

She nodded. "I bought a house with a detached garage that I turned into a shop/showroom for my art. Well, that's what I want to do anyway. It's still a work in progress, but it'll get there sooner or later." Callie thought about the flooring she still had to contract someone to do. As if reading her mind, Jordan spoke up.

"What's left to do in the garage?"

"Flooring is the main thing. Some electrical stuff. I've painted and had the windows replaced, but the other stuff will have to wait a bit." The move alone had cost her a chunk of her savings and she didn't want to start out being in the red.

"I could come take a look, give you some ideas."

This was a side of Jordan she hadn't seen. Maybe beneath the rough outer layer there was a kind soul. "I appreciate the offer, but don't you already have a lot on your plate?" She gathered the remnants of lunch and finished her drink. She'd had a feeling that there was another dimension to Jordan. It was nice to see it was true.

"Having a full plate means less time for random thinking. Unless you prefer I not know where you live." Jordan's mouth twitched.

In the time it took for the words to sink in, Callie had a chance to really study her. Strong features gave Jordan an androgynous appearance at first glance, but the gently arched eyebrows, ridiculously thick and long eyelashes, and the dimples that appeared on the rare occasions when she smiled left little doubt she was a woman. Of course, her body was another story altogether. At least a head taller than her, Jordan overshadowed her. Her shoulders were wide, and her arms were thickly muscled. She either worked out or the work she did provided all the exercise she needed to maintain them. Even sitting relaxed, her thighs strained the material of her jeans. Callie imagined what her body would feel like pressed against her own. Jordan's voice jolted her out of her daydream.

"Callie?"

She shook her head to clear it. "Sorry." It took a second to remember the conversation. "I'd appreciate your input. I don't want to spend a fortune, so I've ignored it, which isn't practical. I need to get it finished so I can set up the space properly." As it was, when the weather cooperated, she brought pieces of glass and whatever else she needed for a job to the shop, leaving her huge stock in totes and boxes in what would eventually become the guest bedroom, if she ever got there. It was such a disaster the way it was now.

Jordan nodded and stood, gathered her trash, and handed the empty bottle to Callie. "I'm free most evenings after six. Let me know what works for you." She started to turn, stopping abruptly. "Thanks for lunch, and the conversation." Jordan's smile seemed tinged with sadness. Or maybe she just wasn't used to smiling.

"You're quite welcome," she said. She meant it. Jordan nodded, but she didn't move, as though trying to find a reason to stay. "Does Thursday work?" Callie wanted to touch her. Brush away whatever caused the glimpse of pain she saw before being replaced by the stoic look she recognized from their first meeting.

"Thursday's fine." Jordan pulled her phone from a back pocket and typed. "Is it the same address as your business card?"

"That's the place." Pleasure rippled through her. Jordan had actually read her card. "I'll cook dinner."

"You don't have to do that." Jordan frowned as she stared at her phone.

Callie stood, needing to be closer. "I want to. It's the least I can do." Her fingers tingled. If this were another woman, she would have grasped her hand, but Jordan wasn't like other women she knew, and she didn't want to fray their tentative truce. Callie was a tactile person, and she liked touching people. But not everyone felt that way.

Jordan glanced up at the deep blue sky, dotted with fluffy white clouds. "Okay. How does six thirty sound?"

"Perfect. Is there anything you're allergic to, or don't like?"

One side of Jordan's mouth rose. "If you feed me tofu, we're done."

She snickered. "That makes two of us. No tofu for sure."

"Enjoy your evening, Callie. I'll see you tomorrow night." Jordan strode in that slow, purposeful way she'd always seen her walk, but she couldn't help thinking her steps seemed lighter. Less burdened. She wondered, as she had no less than a dozen times since that first face-off, what weighed so heavy. Callie was a nurturer by nature and once more she was compelled to help, if only for a little while. She hoped it would be enough.

CHAPTER SIX

Jordan wasn't sure what to make of her behavior. While she often offered to help out strangers...people who didn't know her and likely never would...doing so with someone even vaguely familiar wasn't something she did. She hadn't planned to offer her expertise to Callie, it just happened. It had stung for a minute when Callie hadn't seemed enthused, but why should she be? Their meeting had been anything but friendly and she'd almost thrown Callie out of the house before learning why she was there. Thoughts of her had chased Jordan since that day, but she knew better than to think about a woman in any way other than as a brief, physical distraction.

As she pulled away from the house to head to the commercial building she and some hired crews were rehabbing for a community center, she thought about driving by Callie's to see if she could get a better sense of what she'd gotten herself into, but that was just craziness on her part. She'd enjoyed their lunch together, touched by the kind gesture, especially after their contentious interactions. The feeling that Callie was, by nature, kind and caring was the most plausible reason. And the only one she was willing to entertain.

Jordan drove by the downtown shops, restaurants, and bars. It wasn't long before she noticed a crumpled figure near one of the few vacant buildings. She pulled into the first available spot and jogged to where the figure lay. She bent down, saying a silent prayer that Harry was okay.

"Harry, it's Jory."

When he didn't answer, she gently put her hand on his. The pulse beneath her fingertips was slow, but strong. She gave a little nudge on his shoulder. "Harry, are you okay?" He slowly roused, opened his bright blue, intelligent eyes, and smiled.

"Hi. What are you doing here?" He blinked and glanced around, his smile fading. "Oh. I was dreaming." He rubbed his eyes with the heels of his hands and Jordan helped him sit up.

"I was worried something was wrong and stopped to check on you." She studied his face. "You don't normally sleep in the middle of the business section."

Harry looked around again. "Me and a buddy shared a bottle. I must have passed out." He looked ashamed.

"As long as you're okay. How about a cup of coffee?"

His smile returned. "That would be good."

The convenience store a few doors away had decent coffee. She grabbed a bottle of water and a couple of premade sandwiches before pouring a large cup of steaming brew. After adding two sugars and a generous amount of cream, she brought everything to the counter. While she was being rung up, she spied Harry's favorite candy bar and threw it into the mix.

Harry had moved to the bus stop bench, a place he frequently could be found. "Here you go," Jordan said as she handed him the cup and set the bag beside him.

"That's a lot more than a coffee."

She shrugged. "Just be careful, Harry. You don't like jail, and I don't want to find you there again. Okay?"

He sipped, sighed, and looked up. "Yeah. I know. My bad. I'll make it to the bridge tonight."

They talked for a few minutes about the latest news; Harry read all the discarded newspapers he found. With little else to do for him, Jordan said good-bye. For the last month, she'd been asking Harry to spend the night at her place where he could have a hot shower, a home-cooked meal, and a decent bed. Every time, he'd refused, saying he wasn't as bad off as others and to stop worrying…but she did worry. She might have been too late for her father, but Harry was here, and she would continue to do as much as she could for him. Something about his eyes reminded her of her father's and she wasn't about to ignore a silent plea for help if there was one.

❖

Nervousness wasn't something Callie experienced often. She'd been cleaning and straightening the house and the shop since Jordan's offer to inspect it and give her renovation ideas. The menu had changed twice since then, too. First she'd decided on grilling steaks before thinking Jordan might like a real home-cooked meal and then she pulled out all the stops. She'd splurged a little at the local fish market and picked out two portions of Chilean sea bass. After that, the farmer's market provided a nice selection for the pasta primavera that would serve as both the starch and the vegetable dish. For dessert, she'd reverted to one of her favorite go-to dishes, a lemon pound cake with icing.

She glanced at the clock then hurried to the bedroom to change. She should have planned for another shower, but there wasn't time. After washing her face, she threw on a nice blouse and a pair of capris. It wasn't to impress Jordan, but she didn't want her to think she hung around in sweats and T-shirts all the time. Just sometimes. Callie ran her fingers through her hair and studied her reflection.

"It's not a date, so don't even go there." She nodded once, picked up her lip gloss, and ran it over her lips. Date or not, she wasn't going to stop doing what she'd do in any other situation. Just then, the doorbell rang, and she only stumbled once as she went to answer it.

She smiled as Jordan shifted on her feet and cradled a couple of bottles of wine. Her clothing wasn't all that different from every other time she'd seen her except she appeared freshly showered, her still wet, curly hair framing her face. The dark jeans and solid maroon short-sleeved shirt looked ironed. Pleasure coursed through her at the idea Jordan had gone to such lengths for her. "Hi."

"Hey," Jordan said. "You mentioned dinner, so…" She pushed the bottles forward and gave a tight grin.

Callie took them then set them on the hallway table. "You didn't need to bring anything, but thank you."

"You're welcome." Jordan pointed toward the garage. "Want to show me what you're thinking, and I'll give you my two cents?"

She tapped the remote for the garage door and it rose with only a tiny bit of grinding. Jordan closed her eye at the last screech and stood just outside the opening inspecting the track and the overhead unit. "The newer models are a bit quieter and if you keep the tracks oiled, they won't grind much."

Her face heated. Foolish as it might be, she didn't want Jordan to think she didn't know anything about basic maintenance, even if it was true. "I don't open it except when it's really stuffy in the shop and it'll soon be too cold." She thought about how nice it would be to do something different in its place. "Are there other options?"

Jordan unclipped a small contraption from her belt, pressed a button, and a red laser beam shot to the opposite wall. After measuring the entire space, she turned it off. "Are you planning on being out here year-round?"

Callie nodded. "That's what I bought it for. I'm tired of having half my home dedicated to this." She waved her hand over the workshop side of the space. "Even if it is what I love to do." Jordan appeared deep in thought as she jotted in the smallest notebook Callie had ever seen.

"Heating this much space with a drafty garage door will cost you a fortune. If you install sliders that double fold, you'll save a lot of money and they'll be aesthetically pleasing to customers." Jordan tapped her chin.

Callie had witnessed the gesture more than once and found it adorable.

Jordan pursed her lips. "As nice as the wall color is, you could do with insulation and Sheetrock, unless the temperature doesn't matter for you or the glass."

Before she picked Rehoboth Beach she'd done some serious investigating. The city was fairly temperate all year round, which suited her well, but January and February could still be cold with near freezing temperatures, and with climate change, who knew what the temperatures would be like in the years to come. "It's hard to work when it's below fifty degrees, that's for sure."

"Then insulation is a serious consideration. As for the floor," she said as she walked the length and made a note. "It's in really good shape. There are a few things you could do to warm it up, depending on what you do with the walls, if anything. There's a great surface treatment that will seal it, make it look like linoleum, and keep it from being super slippery if it gets wet."

"What other options are there for the flooring?" She wasn't keen on an industrial look, which was rather odd considering she was using a garage for a showroom.

"Insulate the floor with one or two indoor/outdoor products, then put down a vinyl. You don't want wood out here with it being exposed to the weather. I'd get a couple of mini splits for heat and air conditioning, that way you won't have to block any windows and they're very efficient." Jordan pulled a tape measure off the other side of her belt and quickly measured. "You'll need some electrical work, too."

"What will this cost me?" Numbers were clicking in her head.

"Around twenty-five thousand for all we've talked about, give or take. That would include materials and labor. The good news is that from everything I can see there's no hidden damage. I'll do a quick check on the foundation." She ducked out and disappeared around the side.

Callie dropped onto one of her stools. *Twenty-five grand.* The number soured her stomach. All the items Jordan had highlighted made sense, especially since she wanted to have an inviting place for customers to come and see her work or pick out patterns from the binders she'd amassed in the last six years. But that was a hell of a lot of money. Money she didn't have. Jordan came back in, reattached the tape measure to her hip, and smiled.

"Aside from a couple of minor surface cracks, it's in really good shape."

"Great." The news was better than she might have imagined but it didn't change how much it would cost her to get it into shape. She shook her head before standing. "Let's go open a bottle of wine and discuss details."

"Sounds like a plan to me."

It sounded like a plan to her too, but not exactly what she had in mind when she'd extended the invitation. Not that she'd planned anything at all, of course. It was nothing more than a friendly meal between people who shared a vaguely common interest. She watched Jordan run her hand over the wood doorframe as though examining every inch of it, and her breath caught. *Sure. Nothing more than that.*

CHAPTER SEVEN

Jordan knew attraction when she felt it. Attraction for a woman who had initially pissed her off, then surprised her with kindness wasn't her usual type. The ones who pissed her off were her type because they were the kind of woman she could fuck and walk away from without batting an eye. But Callie was in a different league than those women. She'd been beyond patient when the window had been blocked, and sharing her lunch when Jordan had been in a mood had been an unexpected act of kindness that left her feeling a warmth she didn't often experience. She pushed away any lingering thoughts and concentrated on the reason she was there, not the ones running amok in her head. Callie handed her a glass of red after putting the white in the freezer to chill.

"So. Twenty-five grand, huh?" Callie gestured to the back door and led the way.

Once outside Jordan slowly took it all in. The landscape was a mix of planted beds and patches of wildflowers, which were hard to grow in the sandy soil. The wide covered porch held a loveseat, two chairs with overstuffed cushions, and a framed hammock at the opposite end. She pictured herself there at the end of a long day with a book open on her chest. The house wasn't big and felt more intimate than the four-bedroom rambler that was hers. However, warmth surrounded her because obvious touches from Callie were everywhere she looked. This place felt like a home rather than a location.

"You can lie in the hammock if you want."

Her ears burned. Thinking she was so easy to read was disconcerting. "No, thanks. Just admiring. It's a perfect spot though." She settled into one of the chairs before sipping her wine.

Callie was watching her. A small smile formed. "Why do I get the feeling you're uncomfortable?"

"I wish the numbers were more in line with what you were clearly hoping. I'm giving you options for a full reno, but I can pare it down if you'd rather go in that direction." She would have liked to tell Callie she didn't have to do any of the work, but that wouldn't be practical if she wanted to have her business there. Jordan pulled out the small pad and flipped through pages. When she found an empty one, she produced the miniature pencil and quickly drew a rectangle. "How much space do you need for your showroom?"

Callie sat up, her eyes brightening. "Half would probably do. I want room to hang ornaments and spinners from the ceiling."

Visions of sparkling glass twirling in the bright light meandered through her mind. She drew a few more lines and leaned toward Callie to show her. "This is a scaled down version of what we talked about. This," she said and pointed to a line that divided the rectangle basically in half. "Is a wall that divides the showroom from your work area. I'd still put in the sliders. Not just for the warmth, but to make the space lighter." Jordan pointed to a blank wall. "This might be a good place to put in another window. And you could do vinyl flooring here, but do the other finish in the back, where your workshop will be." She tapped the back half of the rectangle.

After studying the page, Callie looked up. "What about that ugly ceiling?"

"Two options. We could put in decorative rafters throughout, or put an actual ceiling in. Maybe a combination of both."

Callie sat back, took a drink, met her gaze. "We?"

It took a minute for her to catch up. "Uh…well, I could do a lot of the work for you and save you some money. Give you a break as a…as a fellow designer." Jesus, what was she thinking? They'd only just met and now she was offering to do work for her.

"That's a generous offer." Callie continued to sip, her expression a mix of consternation and consideration before she stood. "Let's have dinner. Then we'll talk more about the space and how *we* can design it to be perfect."

She hadn't meant to imply she'd take on the job, but that's what had inadvertently happened. The perplexing part was the idea wasn't dreadful at all. Maybe she could do this. It would be nice to have a goal to share.

❖

The low lights in the dining room gave Callie an opportunity to study Jordan. Once again, she was struck by the opposing parts of her personality. The rough, tough, take no shit side versus the kinder, generous, thoughtful side. When Jordan glanced up and their eyes met, she held the connection while her heart raced.

"This is really good." Jordan's smile reached her eyes.

Callie picked up her wine, more to settle her thoughts than to break the connection. "I'm glad you like it. I considered steak, but that's not really cooking." Jordan tipped her head in question. "It's grilling."

Jordan grinned. "I would have eaten steak. It would have been less work."

"That doesn't matter. I enjoyed cooking the meal." The last time she'd cooked for anyone was more than a month before the move. There'd been no one to cook for since then. Tonight had been a treat in many ways. Jordan's company was at the top of the list. She refused to think about why that was. Jordan clearly kept her distance from people. No matter they'd had some moments of civility bordering on pleasant. Jordan stayed silent throughout most of the meal, though she didn't look uncomfortable. Sensing the need to dispel the silence that separated them, she poured the rest of the wine between their glasses. "If I did the shop like we discussed on the porch, what would that cost, including labor?"

"Rough estimate? Fifteen grand. I'd have to get current material prices to be sure. My part will be minimal. I'd never take more than what you could afford."

Callie mulled over the words. Jordan appeared serious about not overcharging her, but she wouldn't feel good about hiring her because she'd basically thrown in her own labor for free. Maybe there could be a compromise. It was still a large amount, but doable. She'd gotten a woman-owned business grant for five thousand dollars. The rest was in the ballpark of what she'd budgeted and saved up for renovations. When the idea of opening her own shop had formed, rent was the one thing she'd included in her expenses. Finding a house and a retail space in one had been an unexpected bonus. She hadn't meant to stare off into space while she considered what she was going to do, but now she knew.

"When would you be able to find someone to start the work?"

Shock registered on Jordan's face. She put down her empty glass and sat back. "You're serious?"

"Yes. I can't work in an unheated space, and the clutter in the house is starting to annoy me." She leaned forward and rested her arms on the table. "My tolerance for being disorganized is reaching critical mass." She laughed, and Jordan joined her. Callie began clearing the table.

Jordan stood. "I can do dishes," she said as she picked up the bowl of pasta and her own plate.

The muscles in her forearms flexed and Callie's gaze traveled from her wide hand and long fingers, following the cords beneath the deeply tanned skin until they disappeared beneath her shirt. Jordan cleared her throat, and she realized she'd been caught staring. Again. "You're a guest."

Jordan's lips pressed together in a small smirk, her brows knit. "And you cooked. I want to help."

"Fine. You can rinse and stack the dishwasher." They moved in and out of the kitchen in a loop until the table was empty.

"Would you like some pasta to go? I can't possibly eat all this."
She'd made way more than necessary.

"I'll never say no to a doggie bag." Jordan smiled as she
rinsed and carefully set dishes in the rack.

The idea that Jordan would be around a lot if she accepted her
offer had her second-guessing everything. Why was she acting like
a schoolgirl with a crush on the bad boy? Sure, Jordan was rough
and vociferous at times, and Callie tended to like women who didn't
put up with shit from anyone, but the question remained whether
the charming disposition Callie had witnessed tonight was just for
show. Had she witnessed someone whose mood constantly swung
between highs and lows? The impromptu lunch had been her first
chance to see Jordan in a different light. She hoped their current
amicable relationship would continue. She couldn't imagine what
it would be like if they saw each other every day under strained
conditions, but deep down, she had a feeling there was something
special about Jordan. She didn't know why, but her intuition rarely
led her astray. Callie placed the container in a shopping bag. When
she turned, Jordan was leaning against the sink, watching her.
"Would you like some coffee?"

Jordan's gaze trailed down her body, then quickly returned.
"I can't do the flavored stuff." She continued to look at her with
deep intent.

Callie laughed. "I'm not a big fan either, but it is a dark roast."

"Okay then. Coffee sounds good." Jordan did a slow turn.
"Cups?"

"Upper left over the dishwasher." Callie filled the carafe, then
pressed the button to grind the beans. The machine shut off, and
she measured out scoops. Soon the kitchen filled with the aroma of
her favorite scent. "Cream or sugar?"

"Both, please."

The tray she'd bought for carrying items to and from outside
had sat unused since she'd found it at a flea market in her hometown.
She placed the container of various sugar packets on it, then filled
a small pitcher with half-and-half. Jordan brought the mugs over
and added them to the cache.

"How long have you been in the house?" Jordan asked as they waited.

"Three…almost four months." Her family hadn't been on board with the move, but she hoped they'd come around. Thinking it didn't mean it would be so, but maybe if they could see how well she was doing they'd change their minds. Of course, that hadn't been the case so far, but she was making ends meet, and that counted for something. "My parents aren't big supporters of art in general and never understood how I could throw away a chance to use my degree to 'play with broken glass.'"

"What you did to the door is beautiful. I'd hardly call it anything but art. Maybe not a Picasso, but amazing nonetheless."

Callie felt her face heat. She still found it difficult to accept praise for her work. "Thank you."

"It's a nice house."

"Thanks, but you haven't seen much beside the kitchen and living room. It's small, but it's just me, so it's fine."

Jordan shrugged. "I meant it's in good shape." She ducked her head. "Hazard of the trade. Always evaluating the structure of every house I step into."

"Oh."

"Sorry, I didn't mean—"

"It's not what I'd been expected to do, but…" The coffee pot beeped, interrupting her telling of something she rarely talked about. She set the insulated carafe on the tray. Jordan moved to pick it up. "I've got it, but if you could take that covered plate and open the door?" She lifted the tray as Jordan picked up the plate before swinging open the door. Once outside she set it on the table between their seats. Callie poured into each mug, deeply inhaling the rich, roasted scent. "Help yourself," she said. "There's nothing like anticipating a good cup of coffee only to find out it's been ruined by too much of something."

"I'm used to drinking mud," Jordan said as she dumped in a packet of sugar, then added a modest amount of cream. "I'll drink it just about any way, except if it's burnt." She took a tentative sip and hummed her satisfaction. "This definitely isn't mud."

"Glad you like it." Callie hadn't had big expectations for this evening. Surviving an uncharacteristic case of nerves had been the best she'd hoped for. To her surprise, she'd been able to settle down and enjoy her time with Jordan more than she would have believed possible.

"You were talking about the shop not being what you had planned. What was your original plan?" Jordan sat back, looking comfortable and relaxed.

"Use my art degree to teach. It's what my parents expected, and so did I when I started college as a way to achieve that goal." She shrugged.

"Life can't always be planned." Jordan's tone was solemn, shadows darkening her features. "It seems to me that you're doing what you enjoy and that's much more important than following someone else's plan, don't you think?"

She nodded. "That's why I'm doing it. My grandmother was an artist but never had the opportunity to follow her dreams until she no longer had the energy to do so. I don't want that kind of ending for myself." It had been a few months since she'd thought about her grandmother's sacrifice for her family's sake. Foolhardy as it may be Callie wanted to know what Jordan was so desperately trying to hide. "What about you? Have you always wanted to be a general contractor?"

"I was a mason, like my father." Jordan's features turned into a grimace as she inhaled sharply, then stood. "I have to go." She set her mug down as she took a step toward the house.

Callie nearly toppled the tray when she rose to grasp Jordan's hand. "What's wrong?"

Jordan gazed out over the seagrass and past-bloom bee balm, but Callie could tell she wasn't there. She was lost somewhere in a memory, and from the expression on her face, it wasn't pleasant.

Jordan slid her hand away. "I'm sorry. I have to go." She made it to the door before turning to face her. "Thank you for the delicious dinner and wonderful company. I haven't enjoyed an evening like this in a long time."

Callie's heart wasn't usually in play with near strangers. And yet, Jordan didn't feel like a stranger. Once again she was caught off guard by the pull she felt toward her. "You're welcome. If I did something—"

"You didn't. It's all me." Jordan lifted her hand, hesitated, and slowly let it fall to her side. "I'll pull some numbers together for the garage and call you in a few days."

She didn't want Jordan to go. Not like this. "Let me get your food." She grabbed the dessert plate from the table and followed her inside. The slices of lemon cake went into a smaller container and she set it on top of the other, then she knew it was time to say good-bye. Callie handed the bag to Jordan and studied her face. "Are you okay to drive?"

Jordan shared a slow, tentative smile. "Yes. Just a ghost rattling his chain."

When she didn't expand, Callie went with her gut. She stood on tiptoe and placed a light kiss on Jordan's cheek. Warmed by the surprise that registered on Jordan's face and the flush that followed, she smiled. "Have a good night, Jordan."

"Good night," Jordan said, her fingertips briefly touching where Callie's lips had been.

Callie watched her drive away before taking the tray inside. She fixed another cup of coffee then sat on the sofa, thinking. Everyone had their own stuff from the past and that's what everyone brought to the table. Life was messy. She had her own collection of skeletons that she rarely let out of the closet. But Jordan's seemed...heavy. Like a literal weight she carried on her shoulders that others could see rather than holding it close in her heart. Callie rose and went to the garage. She pictured the various things they'd talked about and smiled. Whatever the reason, she wanted more time with Jordan, and now she was going to get it.

CHAPTER EIGHT

Jordan shoved the larger container in the fridge and grabbed a beer, her hand around the neck of the bottle. That's how she felt. Like someone had a hand around her throat, keeping air from expanding her lungs.

She hadn't meant to let Callie see the wound that hadn't healed. Every time she thought she'd made peace with the past the old feelings of betrayal and guilt swirled into her conscience like the harbinger of failure that had become so familiar she considered it a part of herself. Then all the sorrow attached to it overwhelmed her until she couldn't breathe. She'd barely escaped Callie's before breaking down, her shirt still wet with tears. She didn't want or deserve anyone's pity. She owned the pain, like a badge of honor, except there wasn't any honor in the way she'd earned it.

And now she'd agreed to help Callie by not only giving her an estimate, but offering to do most of the work herself. "For Christ's sake." Well, she'd put her foot in it and there wasn't any way to pull free from the mire. She shoved the beer back in the fridge door. The last thing she needed was to get lost in an alcohol haze. Restless from thoughts of the future and tormented by visions of the past, Jordan paced from one end of the house to the other. She didn't mark the passage of time, just the longing for a destination.

When the unsettled energy began to subside, she sat at her desk and began to sketch on graph paper from the measurements she'd taken. Draw, erase, draw some more. Once she was somewhat satisfied with what she saw, Jordan began listing the supplies she'd need. Two-by-fours, drywall, screws, vinyl flooring, more paint, a window, a slider. The list went on and on. She straightened her back and grimaced. The clock revealed she'd been at it for hours. With the passage of time came the calm that always managed to dim the raw energy caused by high emotions.

Jordan stood and stretched. Her bed was calling. She set the coffee for the morning and headed to the shower. While the water turned from chilled to steamy, she closed her eyes and leaned on the tile wall, wanting to hold on to the good moments of her time with Callie. After the awkward start, they'd settled into an amicable conversation. Offering Callie options had been fun, except for the part where her eyes bugged at the estimate. No matter what she decided, there was no getting around needing a heating and air conditioning system. Maybe a semi-vaulted ceiling would serve best, being pleasing to the eye and providing places for glass to dangle and twirl. She liked the image that came to her of Callie standing in the room, sunlight playing over her as the glass pieces moved above.

With the water more to her liking, Jordan soaped her sponge and mechanically scrubbed. She didn't really need another shower, but she felt dirty nonetheless for having marred what up until then had been a pretty perfect evening with a beautiful woman. She shouldn't think of Callie that way, though. The past had proven she wasn't reliable, and Callie appeared to be someone who deserved a person she could trust. The only thing Jordan could be trusted for was doing a good job on a work site and she intended to give her very best.

As she dried off with one of the luxurious towels Mel had given her as a housewarming gift, the idea of spending more time with Callie returned. When she kept the emotional clutter at bay, she could enjoy thoughts of sharing space with her in her element, and the shop was definitely Callie's element. Whenever she talked about her art, Jordan saw the glimmer of excitement dance in her eyes. For Jordan, this was a project where she'd not only see the results of her labor in a short amount of time, but she'd also have the opportunity to do something special for someone who'd shown her kindness and seemed to understand her in a way few people ever did. Callie was special, too, and that was the problem. Jordan wasn't sure she deserved having Callie in her life, but damn if it didn't feel good, and she had no intention of ignoring it, even when she knew it wouldn't last. Nothing good ever did.

❖

The designs Jordan had emailed her were clear and precise. Jordan had put in all the details they'd discussed, right down to the hanging mobiles from the ceiling. The front part of the garage would be transformed into a bright, refined space with an open-concept area with ornate rafters above in the vaulted ceiling where a fan would help circulate heat or air conditioning, but far enough away to not stress the display.

Now that she could envision what it would look like she would give Jordan the go-ahead to begin working on it as soon as possible. Maybe she'd have time to start it after she was finished with the house they were both involved with. It would take Callie another thirty hours to complete the remaining inset windows and the pendants because they were a bit more challenging due to their shape. That meant she'd have time to finish her work before Jordan shooed her out from underfoot. Again. She couldn't help laughing at the memory of a frustrated Jordan when she'd been found in the kitchen.

There were a few details for the garage they still needed to work out, but she had no doubt they'd find a way to make it all work, as long as Jordan didn't try to take over. As it stood now, the back part of the garage was a hodgepodge of the necessities for the projects she was doing. Jigs, tools, folding tables, etc. Pieces of glass were scattered everywhere on haphazard shelves. As much as she enjoyed her art, working in that environment stunted her creativity. It was part of the reason she was having a difficult time completing her orders. There was no *order*. Such was her life at the moment. Hopefully, that would change when the garage was finished. The best-case scenario would be to have the work completed before everything in town closed up for the season, but that was a lofty goal even with Jordan's expertise.

Picturing workbenches at the perfect height, Callie jotted her own notes. She hadn't calculated those items into Jordan's list, but they'd be minimal, she hoped. Another window would be nice back here, too. How much extra would that be? Her phone vibrated and she pulled it from her back pocket. She smiled when she recognized the logo.

"Hello."

"How much of a sticker shock was it?" Jordan chuckled.

Callie laughed. "Not heart attack territory."

"Well, that's good." Jordan paused. "But really, they're okay? Because—"

"Jordan?"

"Yeah?"

"It's perfect. You've nailed it."

Jordan let out a rush of air. "Oh, that's really good."

They set a time to go over the details and things Callie wanted to add. It was nice to have someone show enthusiasm about what mattered to her. Her grandmother had been an artist at one time, but like Callie's parents were with her, Viola got little support from the family, eventually giving up her dreams to be the good wife everyone expected. There was no way Callie would give up her aspirations, not for anyone. She'd make it happen, and prove to them, and to herself, that she had what it took. And in three days, Callie would be one step closer to her dream, and she had one person to thank. Jordan.

❖

"Be sure it's covered. I don't want to have to call you guys back because of sloppy workmanship." Jordan had worked with this crew of painters before, so she knew what they were capable of, but she had to keep an eye on the young ones.

"Sure thing, Jordan. We'll move to the living room next."

She flipped through her notebook. "What color do you have?"

The man pulled a rumpled sheet of paper from his pocket. "Baked Sand," he said proudly.

"You've got three gallons. If you have any left, let me know. The owners are hoping to use it in the downstairs half-bath."

The guy gave her a thumbs-up as he continued rolling. The roofers were next on her list. She climbed the extension ladder and stepped onto the newly-shingled roof. They were just finishing the double garage and she wanted to inspect the ridge vent. As she leaned down, she checked the metal vent to be sure the shingles covered the exposed edge. It was a common place for bats and small creatures to find their way into a home. Satisfied with the result, she went closer and gave the foreman the okay sign. He smiled in return before continuing the bang, bang, bang, bang of shooting roofing nails.

Back on the ground, Jordan was satisfied with the progress, and headed down the driveway until a sound of glass and a few choice curse words reached her. Jordan pinched the bridge of her nose and turned. The front door was open, and her gut told her something was definitely wrong. As she stepped under the overhang and checked the door, she swore under her breath.

The stained-glass window Callie had installed a few days ago had a gaping hole in the bottom left corner. *Son of a bitch.* She looked inside to find a painter with a long-handled roller looking perplexed with his eyes wide in either fear or surprise. She hoped it was fear because she wanted to kill him.

"Boss. I'm sorry. I forgot I propped the door open for more ventilation and when I got to that spot on the wall..." Paul didn't need to explain more.

Jordan ran her hand down her face, dreading having to tell Callie about another fuckup, and this time she'd be the one who would have to fix it. They'd had a good time together the other night and the thought it might come crashing down was upsetting. What's done was done, and she inspected the damage. As someone who knew only the barest about the art, she could see there was at least one piece that would need replacing, possibly two, if it was even possible. "Tape cardboard over the entire window. I'll call the artist."

Paul nodded. "Right away. I'm so sorry about the accident."

She knew what an accident was and what wasn't. Some things happened intentionally, though she was confident Paul hadn't meant to break the window. She strode toward the truck and pulled her phone out, then sat on the open tailgate. The other end rang twice before Callie's chipper voice came on.

"Hey, do you have some wonderful new idea brewing that you want to share?"

She squeezed her eyes. "I wish. The front door glass has some damage. I wanted you to be prepared when you came tomorrow." Jordan prayed she could get through the call without being reamed out.

"Seriously?"

"I'm afraid so." She wouldn't throw anyone under the bus except herself. She was the one responsible for whatever happened on the site, and she'd take the blame. "From what I could tell it looks like only one or two of the small pieces in the corner are damaged."

Callie sighed. "All right."

"Do you think it can be fixed?"

"I'll have to see it first. I've done some repair work before."

The sound of disappointment in Callie's voice tugged at Jordan's conscience. If she could have prevented the accident she would have. It seemed to be a pattern that she was unable to break, even when she tried her best for it to be otherwise. "I'll be here tomorrow after ten. Will you be here before then?"

"Ten is fine." The silence stretched between them. "Thank you for giving me the heads up. I'll see you tomorrow."

Jordan stared at the black screen. She'd tried to turn back time once and it had been an utter failure. She wasn't about to go down that path again. She hoped a worst-case scenario didn't apply here and Callie was able to make the repair instead of having to re-create the whole pane. What Jordan wished for even more was that Callie was still willing to move forward with the garage reno, because if it was otherwise, her disappointment would outweigh her guilt.

CHAPTER NINE

The dreary morning matched Callie's mood. Heavy, gray storm clouds hung low in the sky, casting a pall over the landscape. Rain had arrived late yesterday and continued into the night. Normally, she enjoyed hearing the rain fall on the metal roof of the garage, but last night it sounded more ominous than soothing.

She wasn't looking forward to seeing her hard work in need of repair, if it could be repaired at all. From what Jordan had said, it was a small area in one corner. If there was a bright side to the event, that would be it. Otherwise she'd have to dismantle a whole section and put it back together, but it would never be the same.

For fear of another "accident," she decided to leave installing the pendant shades until all the workmen were gone, then she'd protect each one in a layer of bubble wrap after they were hung. The two remaining windowpanes were carefully nested in the back, wrapped in an old comforter. It was the perfect solution for padding delicate, flat pieces. She also had a few totes full of Styrofoam peanuts for smaller, oddly shaped works, like mobiles and lampshades.

Jordan's truck and one other beat-up car were the only two vehicles at the site. She backed in next to it and took a slow breath after turning off the engine. She didn't want to be angry. Not covering the door insert when there was still a lot going on was careless on her part. She would make sure she didn't make that mistake again. The cost of having to redo pieces because she wasn't paying attention did nothing to ease the worry from her mind. As much as Jordan was around, she couldn't be everywhere, and she'd taken full responsibility for the mishap. Callie barely finished her thought when Jordan appeared at the open garage, an anxious expression on her face. Once she was out of the car, Jordan came closer.

"Hey." Jordan tapped her clipboard against her thigh, much like she had the first time, but her stance was different. As was the former look of annoyance now replaced by embarrassment.

"Hi."

Jordan rocked on her heels. "Want to get this over with?" The wry grin lifted one corner of her generous mouth.

All she could do was nod because what she really wanted to do was either lose her shit by screaming, which really wasn't how she handled things, or hug Jordan in hopes of dispelling her obvious discomfort.

They walked side by side looking down at the ground until Jordan stopped. The glass had been covered on the inside, but she had a clear view of the damage from the outside. Callie pulled a small flashlight from her pocket to make a thorough inspection. One piece of textured red glass had been broken. It ran along the bottom edge of the insert. A dark blue piece, cut in a triangle, sat adjacent to it. She couldn't tell if it was damaged or if the edging had just bent a little from the impact. Either way, it was easily fixable due to the location. After removing the putty and the glazier points she'd remove the whole thing and take it back to the shop for repair. Luckily, she hadn't done anything with the original insert and had brought it with her.

"I'm going to get my tools and take it out, then I'll replace the original until it's repaired."

"I feel awful this happened. Can I help?"

Jordan followed her like a puppy down the walkway. She didn't have the heart to tell her she'd rather she didn't. "Can I trust you to carry the glass?"

"Absolutely." Jordan waited while the hatch opened, appearing eager to please.

"The one in the red towel. The edges are a bit sharp, so grasp it with that. It's slippery."

Jordan's wide hands grasped the edge and eased it out, then she checked her grip. "Where do you want it?"

"Lean it against the wall just inside. The less we have to move it the less chance of it breaking."

Jordan set it down as instructed, then stood with her hands on her hips. "Now what?"

"The cardboard needs to come off, then you can steady the door while I remove the molding."

After carefully peeling away the tape and removing the cardboard, Jordan wedged the door between her feet and held the edge above the door handle. She watched with avid interest as Callie removed the wood trim, then scored the putty before scraping it away with a narrow putty knife. The last step was pulling the glazier points.

"I never knew so much was involved in your work," Jordan said.

"If I want it to not shift and stand up to temperature changes it has to be done right." Callie removed the insert and brought it to the car. Jordan set the original glass into place, and she reversed the process except she used more points and no putty since she'd bring back the repair in a day or two. Once she was satisfied with the temporary pane, she told Jordan she could let go of the door. "Would you mind putting the cardboard over the back? No sense tempting fate."

"Right. Will do." Jordan looked around as though on a mission to show she was there to help. "Is there anything else?"

"I'm going to put in the bathroom and stairway pieces. The pendants aren't going in until the workers are gone, so if you could let me know when they're done, I'd appreciate it." She put her toolbelt on and went to retrieve one of the pieces. Jordan waited on the walkway, her hands shoved deep into her pockets.

"I guess you won't be needing my services for the garage."

"What do you mean?" Callie leaned the window against her hip.

"Why would you want someone who can't keep your work safe to do a project so important to you?"

She carefully set the still-wrapped creation between her feet. "If I gave the impression I'd changed my mind, I'm sorry. If you still want to do the reno, I still want you for the job." Jordan's face showed so much of what she was feeling. Caution. Disbelief. Relief. Finally, she smiled.

"If you're all in, then so am I."

"It's settled then." She hefted the piece. "Do you want to grab a drink tonight to discuss details? I'm craving one of those greasy burgers from that funky pub on Baltimore."

Jordan leaned back. "You like Faraday's?"

She nodded enthusiastically. "I've only been there once and it may have been partially due to being ravenous, but I loved it." They settled on a time and Jordan got in her truck and drove off. There wasn't a real need for getting together except that she appreciated Jordan's honesty, and there was something about her...something sweet and vulnerable that made Callie's heart thump a little harder. The deflated look on her face had been hard to see. Accidents happen. It was no reason to have an attitude toward her. Jordan seemed like a person who was already dealing with a lot, and she didn't want to add to it.

She carried the glass into the master bedroom where a young man was rolling a coat of bluish gray paint on the wall. It was a beautiful, rich color and she could picture how it would frame her art in its soft hue. He stopped and smiled at her. Callie set the glass against the wall, pulled the tape measure from her belt, and checked the opening one more time. Thankfully, the do-over hadn't changed the opening by a discernable amount and she didn't have to worry about too much expansion since it was inside the home.

"Excuse me," the handsome young man said. "Are you the one who did the front door?"

"Yes." She stuck out her hand. "I'm Callie Burke."

"Paul," he said as he shook her hand. "I'm awfully sorry about breaking it. I hope it wasn't ruined."

She sucked in a quick breath. "You broke the door?" she said in disbelief.

Paul paled. "Yes. I forgot I had it open and…" He shrugged. "I'll be sure to stay away from your work. It's really nice." Paul went back to painting.

Callie was left to wonder how much her first impression of Jordan had been skewed. Glimpses of the world Jordan was an active member of included acts of warmth and caring, and a sense of responsibility so deep it was palpable. She wanted to see more of Jordan, the person, not the no-nonsense woman who came across as having to prove herself at every step. Jordan continued to be an enigma that she wanted to figure out, and it was beginning to be more than just idle curiosity.

❖

Jordan laughed because Callie was laughing. Her entire personality was infectious, and she couldn't help liking her. More than like, really. Every time she was around her she wanted to know more about the artist and the person behind the glass. Unlike her own stony stoic surface, Callie reflected joy and light. It shimmered in her eyes like sunstruck glass. Funny how things had changed. When she first saw her standing in the kitchen at the build site she was furious, and now they were discussing how the remodel would go…with Jordan in charge, no less.

"So," Callie said as she finished chewing the last of her burger, the grease running between her fingers while she grabbed her wrinkled napkin before snagging another from the diminished stack. "It kind of sucks that I already painted, but it was a five-gallon special because the color was a mistake."

She couldn't prevent her smile.

"What?" Callie asked.

Jordan sat back, letting the smile bloom. "I noticed. Everyone works within their own color palette, though. I'm not one to judge."

With mostly clean hands, Callie picked up her beer glass and drained the contents. "It's horrible." They laughed again. "That tiny dot of color on the lid looked a lot less like puke than it did on the walls. I won't be sorry to see it go."

"That's good. I'm not sure I could put my name on something that both turns my stomach and hurts my eyes at the same time." Once they had the laughter under control, Jordan picked up the spiral notebook from beside her thigh as she pushed their plates out of the way. "This will be the project bible. There are tabs for easily finding things. Rough sketches. Materials. Order of completion. Notes. That's where you jot things you want to suggest or problem areas you want to discuss. It'll be in the garage most of the time, except if I take it with me to order supplies." She spun the book around so that Callie could peruse what she'd already written. As she flipped through the pages, Jordan took a minute to admire her beauty. Again.

"You're very organized." Callie continued to flip through the different sections.

"Bordering on obsessive compulsive." She shrugged. It got worse after her father was gone. "I've found I worry a little less if I can see it in writing."

Callie's gaze held hers. "Do you worry a lot?"

God, she didn't want to go down this road. Not with Callie. Not when she wanted to hold on to the connection she felt, even if it *was* only one-sided. "Yes." She swallowed hard. "Things can go very wrong, very fast if you're not paying attention to the details."

Callie continued to stare, then reached for her hand. "What went wrong, Jordan?"

Her whole body trembled. She didn't want anyone to see the ugly scar on her heart that had never healed. Maybe it never would. "I can't." It was barely a whisper, and it was all she could do to not let the pain show. Someday if she were lucky, it wouldn't hurt as much as it still did, but the possibility still seemed a long way off. Callie squeezed her hand and she squeezed back.

"It's okay. Just because I want to know doesn't mean I have to." She slid her hand away, then tapped the notebook.

The waitress appeared. "Anything else for you two?"

"Unsweetened iced tea."

"You're trying to kill me, right?" She tried to look annoyed, but the coquettish grin projected back at her made her groan instead. "Coffee," she said to the waitress who smiled knowingly before taking the dishes away. "You were going to say something?"

"Where are you going to start?" Callie played with a scrap of napkin that had been left behind. Her hands were slender with long, tapered fingers. There were a few small nicks on her fingertips, and she wondered if Callie ever noticed them as she worked.

"I'd like to start at the back and work my way forward. The current garage door will be useful for delivering materials, so it will be one of the last things to go. I don't want to order the sliders until I know the exact size needed. If we can get stock, it'll be cheaper."

"Is there any custom stuff in the plans right now?"

It was a reasonable question. "I haven't earmarked any, but that's up to you." The waitress set their drinks down, along with the bill.

Callie unwrapped her straw, swirled the lemon wedge, then sipped. "Maybe lighting, but I don't want to go nuts with it either. I'll have a better idea once some of the interior is done. I'm having a hard time picturing the results." Her laugh was a bit sarcastic. "That's really not something I should be advertising since a lot of my pieces are custom works based on things I visualize."

The idea that Callie thought she was lacking in any way didn't sit well. "You had a vision and I've disrupted it. I'll try not to mess with it too much." She'd gotten a bit overzealous when she'd looked at the space and envisioned what it could be.

Waving her off, Callie pushed the half-empty glass away. "Don't be silly. I know it will be great."

She hadn't been "great" at anything in a long time, but she wasn't about to blow her chance. Especially knowing it meant so much to Callie. Not to mention that she wasn't about to blow her chance at spending more time with her, either.

CHAPTER TEN

After their discussion the prior week, Jordan had estimated she'd begin the work this week, giving her time to order materials and close a job or two that was wrapping up. She'd called Callie last night to say she could start the following day, if that was okay, and Callie couldn't wait to get the project under way.

In preparation of Jordan's arrival, she needed to move her supplies out of the shop and into the house, something she was dreading, but without anyone else to rely on, it was up to her. The cart she'd purchased a while back would come in handy and she was glad there wasn't more than the six totes and random items from her workbench to schlep from one place to the other. Her completed items were another story, though there were less than two dozen and she'd managed to get those into the house in six trips. The heavy stuff was up next, and she decided to take a break before starting the heavy hauling. Callie sat on her back steps drinking water and contemplating how she'd arrived at today.

She chose Delaware to escape the heat and humidity of Florida, wanting to experience the tepid, year-round temperatures it offered. Ever since her family had moved south when she was twelve years old, she'd had a hard time acclimating and didn't understand why people wanted to live there. Aside from the threat of hurricanes and the never-ending summer, there were bugs. Huge, disgusting, hard-to-kill bugs. Just thinking about them gave her the willies.

The tourist season, which was already in full swing, would be busy and likely her most lucrative time, though commission orders might come in often enough that she would survive the winter without having to scrimp. If she had to, she could always teach a class or two. For practicality's sake, she'd completed the Delaware requirements for certification for elementary and middle-school teaching before moving. Just because glass art was her dream didn't mean she could throw caution to the wind and chance being broke and homeless. There were risks to any new adventure, and ignoring possible failure was foolhardy.

But Callie wasn't a fatalist either. She was looking forward to the work to be done on the garage, even if it did mean her car would be exposed to the weather. If all went well, there was a future plan to build a single-car garage between the house and shop, though farther back so as to not ruin the view. Not that she had much of one. If she stood at the far corner of the front porch and the streets were quiet, she could hear the ocean. At least, that's what she told herself.

Her home was in a residential area dotted here and there with a few funky little shops like hers, and located just a few blocks from the boardwalk. Because the area was so walkable, location wasn't as crucial as it might be in other tourist areas. Seasonal rentals were plentiful, as were the short-term vacationers who strolled along the side streets in search of hidden treasures like that quirky little pottery stand a few blocks over, and she was optimistic her shop would be considered a treasure find, too. Luckily, there weren't any other artists like her in Rehoboth Beach, and she'd already spoken to a few of the gift shops about displaying some of her work as well as agreeing to distribute her business card. Most were open to the idea because a sale for her was also a sale for them, and the 60/40 split was the going rate.

The clock displayed a few minutes past eight. Unlike the first few weeks since she'd met Jordan, the last week had dragged on. Even with the pendants to keep her busy, anticipation ran along her nerves. Whether it was because she was one step closer to her dream or wanting to see Jordan again, Callie wasn't sure. If there was one thing she would admit to, it was knowing Jordan wouldn't cut corners or try to take advantage of her because she was a woman. Firing the first Realtor she'd worked with had been justified. She hated his condescending attitude, and he'd treated her as though she knew nothing about real estate or property values. She'd done her homework when the hunt for a location had begun.

Once Jordan started, she'd have to work solely in the guest room, and she hoped it would be short-term. She didn't like having her personal space invaded by her work, even if she was passionate about the art she created no matter where she did it. There was something about keeping the two separate that was important to her.

The sound of an engine in the driveway sent her pulse into overdrive. She started to run to the front door. "Stand down," she said under her breath. Jordan was there in a professional capacity. There was nothing to get excited about. That little fact did nothing to calm her excitement. Ready for what lay ahead, Callie pushed through the screen door and greeted Jordan who had raised the garage door. She had two remotes and insisted Jordan take one.

"Good morning."

Jordan slid her sunglasses onto her head. "That it is." She glanced at the sky, then into her eyes. "You ready for this?"

She held her breath as she took in one of the sexiest butches she'd ever met. Remembering she'd been asked a question, Callie nodded enthusiastically. They'd negotiated terms for their agreement. Callie would do what she could to help, and Jordan would allow her to use tools once she showed her how. "Where do we start?"

"Let's make sure everything is out of the garage. One piece of broken glass was enough for me." Jordan's lopsided grin looked good on her.

"There are a few things I couldn't carry into the house alone, and there's a tote that's really heavy." She pointed to the offensive bin. "We should be able to lift it together."

Jordan studied it. "Let me give it a try." She bent with her knees, grabbed the handles, and lifted. "Not too bad. Where do you want it?"

She hurried ahead to open the door. "In the guest room." The house wasn't huge. It didn't need to be. It was just her and maybe a pet someday, but the two-bedroom, two-bath bungalow was perfect. The only problem was the majority of storage space was in the basement and she didn't want to be lugging her materials up and down that narrow staircase as often as she needed things. For a couple of months, if that's what it took, she'd manage. As Jordan passed by, Callie got a closer view of the well-developed muscles in her arms. Not for the first time, she pictured those arms extended above her and Jordan's solid weight pressed to hers. She had to push those thoughts away. Jordan hadn't shown any interest in her, other than helping with the project. Her business had to come before any kind of crush as well. So much of her preferred career had taken a back seat to practicality that she was ready to surge toward her goal with the same gusto she'd had when it came to finding her own space.

The rest of the move went quickly. There hadn't been too much left after she'd done what she could. What remained had been the heavier things she couldn't move alone, though Jordan had managed most of them single-handedly.

"Would you like coffee or something cold to drink?"

"Thanks. I'm good for now, though I'll probably take you up on the offer later." Jordan dropped the tailgate of the truck and began pulling tools from the bed.

Callie pointed to the objects lined up in neat rows, most of which she could name. "Can I help?"

"If you don't mind getting dirty you can."

Deciding to ignore the potential double entendre, she began picking up stuff she could easily handle. When she reached for the level, Jordan's hand closed over it first.

"Sorry. This is..." Jordan visibly struggled to go on. "Was... my father's. It's not fragile but—"

"It's precious to you. I understand." She couldn't imagine what the pain of losing a parent would feel like because she still had hers. As she'd grown older, the gulf between them had widened, mostly because they considered themselves to be above blue-collar workers, a much different attitude than Callie had for anyone who was willing to work for a day's wage. But they were her parents, and she wasn't so alienated that she didn't care. She loved them from a distance, and that was how she liked it. Callie stepped back and Jordan lifted the level with reverence before taking it inside. Maybe this was the shadow that never quite left Jordan's eyes.

❖

Once the garage was empty except for her tools, Jordan unrolled the blueprints on the tailgate.

"This indicates where the sliders will go." Jordan pointed to a section of dissecting lines. "This area is the shop, and this is the workspace." The shop was slightly smaller than the working space due to the details Callie had requested. "These are the rafters." She glanced up. The exposed rafters were evenly spaced out and carefully measured to look aesthetically pleasing. Even though they were ornamental rather than structural was no reason for sloppy planning. Callie appeared overwhelmed. "Is something wrong?"

Callie continued to stare at the paper before meeting her gaze. "How do you make sense of it all? There's so many marks and lines and numbers."

"Practice." She smiled. "Lots and lots of practice." For the first time since meeting her, Callie looked completely lost. "It's okay. You don't have to understand it all. That's why you have me." The blueprint class she'd taken had been daunting at first, but once she got the hang of it and had a grasp of what each line and symbol meant, she'd enjoyed it immensely. There was nothing like being organized down to the minutest detail.

"Good thing. Otherwise there'd be a ton of wrong shit where it didn't belong." Callie's cheeks turned pink.

"Even I do that on a rare occasion." She met Callie's gaze and lost herself for a moment in the soft green of her eyes. "I'll do all I can to make sure that doesn't happen on this project." Callie lightly touched her forearm, sending a shockwave all the way to her clit. That wasn't supposed to happen.

"I'm not concerned. You've already proven you make things right in the end, so don't worry so much." Callie's gaze flicked from hers to her lips and back again before she slid her hand away. "So, can we start?"

Just then, a flatbed truck slowly cruised down the street and stopped along the curb. She nodded in its direction. "Perfect timing. Staging materials is next." Jordan had the foresight to include a forklift in her order. The street was too narrow for a semi to back in the driveway and there was no way they could move all she'd ordered by hand. That would take all day.

Callie's excitement was palpable. She clapped her hands together. "What can I do?"

"Stay out of the way and watch." She saw the flash of disappointment on Callie's face and quickly added, "Because the boom can move erratically, and I don't want you hurt." Jordan met the driver on the sidewalk and gave instructions as to what items she wanted where. This was only the first of what would probably be at least one more delivery. If she'd ordered everything she needed now, she'd have no room to work. It didn't take long for the materials to be unloaded in the driveway and she used the forklift to move a pallet of two-by-fours that she needed for framing inside. She turned to an expectant Callie as the truck pulled away. "Now the fun begins." The words would have rung true even if she wasn't standing next to a beautiful woman. She enjoyed her craft, and Callie being on the project had nothing at all to do with her anticipation.

CHAPTER ELEVEN

Jordan wiped the sweat from her brow with the hem of her T-shirt. It had been a long day and she was more than ready for a hot shower, a cold beer, and a meal. She surveyed the results of their combined labor. Callie had been an enthusiastic assistant, even when she floundered a time or two with not understanding a concept or the name of a tool. And she never complained about the heat or the heavy lifting or the loud equipment. Jordan had even shown her how to use the chop saw after cautioning her against using it incorrectly. The wide-eyed expression on her face had been priceless.

Callie came bounding out of the house showered and changed into comfortable looking capris and a short-sleeved shirt. "Want to grab a bite to eat? I'm starving."

They'd only stopped for hydration a couple of times and a piece of fruit around midday. Jordan wasn't much on interruptions when she worked unless absolutely necessary. "I'm a mess."

"I don't think so, but you could probably use a shower." Callie smiled, reached up, and picked a few wood chips from her hair.

Jordan caught her hand. Her head screamed what a bad idea it was to pretend Callie found her attractive in any way other than her building skills. "Only if you let me treat." Did she just insinuate they were going on a date?

"Deal."

Well, that was easy enough, and there didn't seem to be an implication of anything more than just two people eating food together. Great. Jordan motioned to the truck. "Unless you're into grunge, we're going to my house so I can shower and change first." Callie jumped in as Jordan opened the door. "Do you need anything from the house?" She pressed the remote and the garage door trembled down with a grind. She'd be glad when the noisy contraception was gone.

Callie produced her cell phone and keys. "I travel light."

"Good enough." As she rounded the truck, a common mantra marched through her head. *What the fuck am I doing?* She promptly ignored it.

❖

"Make yourself at home." Jordan flicked on lights and dropped her keys on the hallway table. She went to the fridge and grabbed a couple of waters, then downed one. As the cold quenched her thirst then exploded in her belly, the old familiar feeling of having done her best today enveloped her. It had been a long time since she'd felt that way. She lifted her gaze and met Callie's, her head tipped. "Want one?" She held out the remaining bottle.

"I'm good."

She put it back in the fridge. "I won't be long. Want the TV on?"

"I'll just snoop, if that's okay."

She laughed hard. "Just don't look in the hall closet." She leaned close. "That's where the bodies are hidden." Jordan didn't have a clue if Callie thought she was kidding or not, but if she was still there when she was done with her shower, chances were she had a great sense of humor.

Twenty minutes later and glad to be rid of the sweat and sawdust, Jordan strode into the open living and dining room. Callie stood just beyond the patio doors, the shape of her body outlined in the low sunshine. Jordan's body stirred with arousal, her belly tightened with desire. There wasn't much she could do to stop it. It had been months since she'd been with a woman. Ignoring the sensations assaulting her, Jordan slid the screen back and stepped into the warm evening air.

"Nothing's missing in the house and you're still here. Guess I can trust you well enough."

Callie grinned. "So that's all it takes to gain your trust. Not stealing from you?"

Was that all it took? Should life and relationships be as simple as not taking from the other person what they weren't willing to freely give? Maybe all this time she'd been expecting too much. "It helps." Jordan couldn't miss the curiosity in Callie's eyes. "Ready for some food?"

"And a drink. We both deserve one."

"I think you're the one who really deserves that, but I'm not going to pass on one myself." Jordan locked the back door before they moved through the house to the front. She had no idea what she was doing, but that didn't mean she couldn't find a bit of respite in this beautiful woman's company for a few hours.

❖

Callie looked out the open window, enjoying the pleasant temperature and the company beside her. It had been a busy, productive day and the progress made her happy. It was so wonderful that Jordan was happy to let her help. Being involved was better than watching from the sidelines. And watching Jordan work had been a symphony of motion. Her movements were calculated, and she didn't waste energy. Her body revealed years of memorized motion and deeply defined muscles. She was strong, too. Callie pictured being lifted by her, laid on a bed of fresh linens, then taken to a physical place of Jordan's making. Unable to stop herself, she let the images fill her and she embraced the stirrings inside her body. Soft curses drew her attention.

"I guess everyone decided to come to town tonight."

The main thoroughfare was packed with cars and people milled about in groups or strolled at a leisurely pace. Even though Labor Day had just come and gone, the weather remained a beautiful mix of warm days and cooler nights. She scanned for a parking space, but all the cars ahead of them were doing the same thing. "I don't think you're going to find anything."

"Plan B," Jordan said as she flashed a heart-stopping smile at her. "You might want to remember this." They made a quick left, went two blocks, then turned right. The truck moved along at a slow pace until they spotted an opening, but she wasn't sure the truck would fit. Callie didn't say anything. Obviously, Jordan thought she could make it work. She backed into the spot with a few maneuvers and a couple of feet to spare. "Hope you don't mind walking a bit."

More than a little impressed with her parking skills, Callie grinned. "Not at all. Especially since you shared your wisdom about side streets."

Jordan met her on the sidewalk. "Did you have a place in mind to go to eat?"

"Not really." She was still getting to know her neighborhood and hadn't ventured off the main drag.

"Good. I'll show you one of my favorite places."

They turned down the next block that ran parallel with Rehoboth Ave. It too was crowded, and Jordan slipped her hand into Callie's as she led the way through a throng of people gathered outside a patio bar. They turned another corner and Jordan abruptly stopped. She peered around her and looked in the direction of Jordan's gaze. A homeless man sat on the sidewalk between an empty shop and a convenience store, an assortment of bags piled next to him. Teen-aged boys stood a few feet away laughing and pointing. She couldn't quite make out what they were saying, but from the look on Jordan's face, it wasn't nice.

"Hey, what are you doing?" Jordan moved forward quickly after letting go of Callie's hand and stood between the hecklers and the man sitting quietly on the ground.

"We're talking to the old dude. What's it to you?"

Jordan's hands clenched into fists at her sides. "Show some respect. This man has a name. He's a father, a husband, and an ex-Marine. What have you done in your life so far?" The boys grumbled but moved on. Jordan knelt next to the man. "Hey, Harry. You okay?"

Callie stood back, awed that Jordan had stepped in and even more surprised that she knew the man's name.

"Doing okay, Jory." He winked and smiled through cracked lips. "Where you been?"

Jordan glanced away. "Working. What about you? You staying safe?"

Harry cackled. "Told you not to worry about me. I make do." He patted his pile of belongings fondly.

"How about a coffee?" Jordan asked.

"That would be nice."

Jordan lightly touched his shoulder before rising and moved to where Callie stood anchored on the sidewalk. "Do you mind waiting a few more minutes?"

"Not at all." Callie watched Jordan duck into the convenience store before she lowered herself to the ground near Harry. "Hi, I'm Callie." She extended her hand. He stared at it, looking surprised, before firmly shaking.

"You Jory's gal?"

The inference was endearing. Something about the sparkle in his eyes when he said Jordan's name touched her, warming her insides. "We're just friends."

"Uh-huh." Harry studied her with an intensity that probably came from years of observation. "But you'd like to be more."

The question took her back to a few minutes earlier when Jordan had so naturally taken her hand. Did she want more with Jordan? Was there any interest on Jordan's part? Her thoughts were interrupted by Jordan's return. Jordan went to one knee until she and Harry were eye level again.

"Here you go." Jordan handed him a large cup of steaming coffee. She placed a paper shopping bag next to his pile. "Some water."

Harry peeked inside. "There's more than water in here." He reached in and brought out a hot sandwich.

Jordan shrugged. "It's not the kind you like. I'll come by in a few days and snag you one." She handed him a wad of napkins, a couple of wet wipes, and a knife and fork.

Harry's eyes were glassy. "Jory, you don't have to do that."

"I want to. That's what friends are for." She clasped his shoulder and smiled. "Be careful. Be safe. Be smart." Jordan stood and helped Callie to her feet as well.

"Be wise. Be brave. Be open," Harry said, then winked.

Jordan nodded before placing her hand on Callie's back and guiding her down the street.

❖

"I hope I didn't get in the way today." Callie had enjoyed having a hand in the construction of her future business, and she hoped she hadn't been a hindrance.

"Don't take this the wrong way, but I was surprised at how well you did." A lopsided smile formed. Jordan set down her Moscow Mule.

She chuckled. She'd encouraged Jordan to have "one drink" in celebration of a good day's work. "I take it you didn't think that would happen?"

"Anything's possible. I went into it with optimism, and you exceeded expectations." Jordan lifted her glass in a toast. "I may hire you."

She choked on her drink and covered her mouth with her hand. She concentrated on swallowing and managed to only cough a few times. "Not that I don't think I'd learn a lot, but construction isn't a career goal for me."

"That's too bad, I could use a good assistant."

"Uh-huh." She ran her fingertip around the rim of the glass, making it sing. Jordan picked up a menu from the middle of the table and handed it to her. It was one of the wooden placard type, with the menu varnished over on the front and back. The smooth, clean surface was a nice surprise. "What do you recommend?"

"I've never had a bad meal here. What are your taste buds screaming for?"

The words "your mouth" almost shot out, but she reined them in at the last second, pretending there was a residual cough. "Maybe an appetizer and a light entrée?"

Jordan looked in deep thought. "I should have asked if you liked seafood?"

"All except salmon. You don't have to worry though, I can always find something."

"I don't want to be presumptuous, but I'd like to order the appetizers if that's okay?" There was that look of discomfort that seemed to follow Jordan wherever she was.

Callie put the menu down and smiled. "That would be nice. I like take-charge women."

Jordan's cheeks colored. She glanced up and searched the restaurant, then nodded at the waiter who'd just delivered a meal to the table behind them. "Ms. Spade? It's a pleasure to see you again. What can I get for you?"

"Hello, Dell. We'd like the crab dip and the roasted brussels sprouts."

"Very good. Another drink?"

"I'll stick with this one. Callie?"

She looked at her near empty glass. "Well, since you're driving, why not?"

Dell nodded and disappeared. More than once Callie had wondered about how many people seemed to know Jordan. Had she lived in the area for a long time or were people familiar with her because of the business she was in? It was all so different from being in Florida where neighbors were often transient or snowbirds who were there for the winter months, then gone to more temperate parts of the country for summer. "How long have you been friends with Harry?"

A small smile graced Jordan's lips as she sipped the last of her drink. "About four years. I found him in the dumpster on a jobsite." She must have revealed the shocked horror she felt and Jordan hurried to explain. "He was looking for bottle returns. I hauled his ass out of there and handed him a five. There was all kinds of debris in there. He could have been seriously hurt."

Callie studied Jordan's small crow's feet, the lines in her forehead, and her ruddy complexion. She'd tried to guess Jordan's age before, and while it didn't really matter, she couldn't help wondering at the type of experiences she'd had to make her come across as older than she likely was. "You care about him."

Jordan met her gaze. "I do. He doesn't have anyone else that does. His family couldn't handle his PTSD and he left to save them from suffering his uncontrollable mood swings. Everyone should have someone to look after them." Sorrow filled her eyes, but Callie didn't think it was for Harry. "Everyone needs someone to lean on now and again. It doesn't mean Harry isn't capable though." Dell slid her drink in front of her and set down the dishes Jordan had ordered.

"Can I get you anything else?" Dell asked Jordan as he took the empty mug.

"Seltzer with a cranberry splash." Jordan gestured to the plates. "Dig in."

As refined as the restaurant was, Jordan was the opposite, but it fit her personality better than putting on airs. She'd never found the austerity of those high-born types to be appealing. It was one of the things that really annoyed her about her family. She'd much rather be considered down-to-earth than a snob. "It looks delicious." She scooped some dip onto her plate and set a piece of toasted bread beside it before adding the brussels sprouts. "I've never had these roasted."

Jordan added a helping of each to her plate. "That's a shame. Roasting gives them a nutty quality. And the dip is the best I've found anywhere."

Jordan watched as she stabbed a sprout then slid it off the fork. When she chewed, a flavor explosion burst forth. "Wow, this is good." She glanced surreptitiously at Jordan who grinned as she dug into her own food.

"Mm-hmm. Glad you like it." Jordan took a bite of crostini and dip, then washed it down with her seltzer. "What brought you to the booming metropolis of Rehoboth?"

"When I decided to try my hand at starting my own business, I didn't really have a destination in mind other than getting away from the constant heat and ongoing threat of hurricanes in Florida." Callie had never warmed to the idea of it being her forever home.

"You didn't like your home state?" Jordan asked after wiping her mouth on the linen napkin that she'd draped on her lap.

"I started searching for temperate vacation destinations where there'd be an influx of visitors, which would be good for selling my craft, but also a place that had a good vibe." She groaned, rolling her eyes and laughing. "What a fiasco that was. I ended up down the internet rabbit hole more than once."

Jordan laughed in response. "It's an easy hole to tumble into. I stay away as much as I can." After a brief pause, she went on. "How long ago did you decide to leave home?"

Even more than when she first arrived, Callie was sure she'd made the right decision. "Florida was never my home state. It was my parents' decision to pull up roots and move to where all the "important people lived.""

Jordan gestured to the waiter, who removed the minute remnants of their apps and returned with menus. "Why don't we order, then you can tell me more." Jordan studied her. Her eye color, which was usually honey brown, had streaks of gray and green.

Callie's body reacted to the intensity of Jordan's gaze. Was the attraction that tugged at her something Jordan also felt? God, this wasn't the time to get lost in Jordan fantasy land. She sipped her wine and concentrated. Every dish sounded delicious, but she wasn't starving anymore, and decided on a chopped salad with shrimp while Jordan chose ling fish and pumpkin tagine, a dish she'd never heard of.

Jordan handed off her menu and waited until they were alone. "Now that we've taken care of our bellies I'd like to hear more about how you got here."

"It made sense to make a list of important amenities and those that didn't really much matter. At the top of the list was being near the ocean, but without the kind of heat Florida had."

"This area has a lot to offer, though it can get hot for a few days. August can be intense some years, but it doesn't last."

"It wasn't all horrible. I liked the sound of the ocean and the feel of warm sand between my toes, but the humidity was more than unpleasant." She thought a bit more about what had compelled her north. "I liked that there was a fairly large art community here, especially since where I lived people didn't consider art that cost less than a hundred thousand to be 'art' worthy." She made air quotes before realizing how bitter she sounded, probably because she was, at least a little. Not to mention she detested being invited to social events where they would only talk about her teaching degree, like the bachelor's in art she'd earned in addition meant nothing. All the while her parents nagged at her to keep going until she had a PhD, insisting that she'd never be qualified for college instruction or considered for promotions without it, as though being an elementary or high school teacher was below their status. That rising through the ranks to tenured professor was more befitting her upbringing. Just one more reason for getting away from their critical appraisal. Their entrees arrived, jarring her back to the present. "I came to Delaware because I thought I could be happy here for a long time."

"Are you? Happy I mean?"

Callie hadn't given much thought to her emotional state since the move. There was always so much going on, so much to do. She was sure of one thing though. "I'm happy right now, enjoying this lovely dinner with a very handsome woman." Even in the soft lighting she saw Jordan's cheeks darken. For as rough as Jordan could be, Callie enjoyed catching glimpses of a softer side, like watching her interactions with Harry. Those few moments they'd spent together were telling, and Harry's fondness for her was so obvious. She was beginning to understand why.

"You're a sweet talker," Jordan said gruffly, her eyes darting around as if unable to meet hers.

"Maybe, but I'm serious." She would have touched her then, to show her in some small way that she meant it, but Dell made an appearance, the moment lost.

"How is everything?"

She'd been so caught up in her thoughts and the ongoing conversation with Jordan, she hadn't even tasted her food.

She stuck her fork in and took a small helping. When she looked up Jordan's eyes sparkled in the flickering candlelight. "It's perfect," she said.

"Would you like more wine, miss?"

She giggled at the term, then caught her lower lip in her teeth. "I'm not sure I should."

"I'm not having any more alcohol. I'll see that you get home safely." Jordan's eyebrow quirked.

"Oh, why not." She laughed.

"That's the spirit."

She didn't usually have more than one drink, especially when she was on a date. Wait. Was this a date? It felt like a date. Their interactions were date-worthy stuff for sure, and she was confident Jordan was a lesbian, but looks weren't always a definitive indicator. One thing was certain, she needed to remember why they were sitting at the table together tonight, and it had nothing at all to do with her attraction for Jordan.

She'd put off pursuing her dream long enough, thanks to the lack of support she'd received from her family, and the way they had her questioning her own abilities. Those doubts still troubled her in the early hours of the morning when she was tossing and turning, and they occasionally slipped in when she made a mistake, their voices loudly proclaiming her ineptness at knowing how to run her own business. They were adamant that leaving her family behind and not pursuing a higher degree to "follow a fancy that would likely prove to be a huge mistake" was one reason she was determined to show them she could make a living doing what she loved. Getting emotionally involved at this point would only serve as a distraction. A very handsome one, but a distraction nonetheless.

CHAPTER TWELVE

Jordan slowed the vehicle in the driveway and stole a glance at Callie. She was sure the last drink had given her quite the buzz, because she'd giggled and laughed as they chatted through the rest of dinner. Not that she minded. Callie was light spirited most of the time, and it was one of the reasons Jordan enjoyed her company. The downer syndrome Jordan had immersed herself in was slowly lifting and she needed to remember to enjoy the things that were given to her as gifts. In her opinion, Callie was one.

"Let me come around and help you out."

"I'm fine." Callie slapped the seat and giggled again.

She unbuckled her seat belt. "Stay there, please?" Jordan hopped out, not trusting Callie to do as requested. Lucky for her, she reached the other side just as Callie slid out. Luckier still, she was able to catch her and set her on unsteady feet but held her close. *God, she feels good.*

"Whoopsie." Callie's arms moved up her shoulders, her hands locking behind her neck.

She inhaled the citrus scent of her hair and resisted running her fingers through the thick, soft waves.

"I knew three was overkill." Callie hiccupped and pealed laughter.

Staying in this position was foolish. Her clit was already swollen from the brief contact. Jordan gently pried her hands from her neck, then wrapped her arm around Callie's waist before guiding her to the front door. "Where's your keys?"

"Right here." Callie shoved her hand into her pocket and came up empty. "Hmm." She tried to get her hand into the other side. After two unsuccessful tries, the task appeared too much and she sagged against Jordan with a sigh, her eyes closed.

Jordan silently groaned. Left with the choice of standing outside all night, she asked, "May I?"

Callie scrunched her nose and finally realized what she was asking after she pointed to the offensive pocket.

"Oh, sure." Callie thrust her hip forward as she leaned into her for support, and Jordan's pulse quickened.

Desperate to get her inside, she quickly located the small lump and dove in. In any other circumstance she would have reveled in having her fingers so close to Callie's skin, but this wasn't the night to have those longings surface. She retrieved the ring with two keys and let out a breath though her heart and clit pounded in synchronized rhythm. Jordan focused on the task of the moment rather than the ensuing frustration that would follow once she had Callie settled. She slipped the key in the lock and prayed as she continued to hold Callie upright. The door swung in when she turned the knob.

"Magic," Callie whispered as she pressed her hand to the center of Jordan's chest. "I knew you were magic."

Ignoring the pleasure that coursed through her, Jordan guided Callie inside. "I think you should lie down."

"Oh yeah," Callie said.

She tried not to stare into those damnable green eyes. Even a bit hazed, they were such a calm and vibrant color, and it was all she could do not to kiss her, alcohol be damned. But Jordan wasn't that selfish person anymore. The one who would take advantage of a situation for her own benefit. "Bedroom?"

Callie spun toward the hallway and the motion sent her swaying. Jordan caught her before she careened headfirst into the wall. She picked Callie up and headed toward the back of the house. The second door on the right revealed a bedroom. Airy curtains hung from the windows and ocean art dotted the walls. The bed was neatly made and crisp looking. Game plan in place, she carefully set her down and reached for the covers with her free hand before turning her to sit. Jordan went to her knee to remove Callie's shoes and Callie's fingers dragged through her hair, sending a shiver down her spine.

"I knew it would be thick." Callie continued to stroke. "Like your arms." Her fingers trailed down the back of her head, over her shoulder to her forearm, and her muscles tensed beneath Callie's probing fingers. "How did they get so big and strong? I like looking at them."

Oh, God. She needed Callie to stop touching her. "Why don't you lie down and relax?"

"I'm a lesbian." Callie patted the bedding beside her and smiled lopsidedly. "Are you going to join me?"

"No." Jordan was doing all she could to ignore Callie's body because it had curves in all the places that Jordan found so damn sexy.

"Huh. I could have sworn you were a lesbian."

"Why don't you close your eyes? I'll go get you a bottle of water and then we'll talk about it." She didn't want to talk about it. If she talked to Callie about her orientation she wanted her rational and sober, not three drinks in. Jordan walked through the neat space with the little touches of lived-in clutter. Unopened mail on the counter. A stack of magazines strewn on the coffee table. A coffee cup in the sink. Much like her own house. Not unkept, but not sterile either. With a bottle of water in her hand, she tried to come up with some plausible reason to leave that wouldn't hurt Callie's feelings. When she reached the bedroom doorway, her anxiety dwindled. Callie lay with her eyes closed, the steady rhythm of her breathing indicating she was asleep and giving Jordan the perfect opportunity to sneak away. Yet the unpleasant tightness...that familiar feeling of abandonment...tried to linger and she pushed it away.

Jordan went into the bathroom and opened the medicine chest, hoping not to see any of the private stuff Callie might have there. She found the bottle of ibuprofen and scooted out like she had been caught with her hand in the candy jar. Quietly chuckling, she set the bottle next to the water, then moved to wipe a curl off Callie's face before thinking better of it. If she woke…if she looked at Jordan again with the unmistakable longing she'd recognized earlier… she might not be able to resist. Pausing at the door, she looked at her one more time before switching off the light. She didn't really want to leave, but staying wasn't an option. Callie didn't really know her. If she did, she might not have agreed to let her get as close as she had, and there'd be no one to blame but herself.

❖

Sunlight streamed through the open window and fell across the foot of her bed. Callie glanced down along her body. She was fully clothed. And wrinkled beyond salvage. She smiled when she flipped over. The bottle of water and ibuprofen had to have been left by Jordan. Sitting up abruptly hadn't been wise on her part. Neither was getting tipsy at dinner. While she hadn't been fall-down drunk, there were parts that were a bit fuzzy. The evening had been fun and relaxing, even a bit flirty, until after dinner. That's when the night lost its sharp edge.

She needed a shower. And coffee. She took two pills to ward off any lasting effects, dragged herself from bed, and plodded to the kitchen. The clock on the microwave displayed seven twenty, much later than she normally slept. She'd worked alongside Jordan all day yesterday and wasn't used to that type of physical activity. After she filled the carafe, then measured coffee, she heard a vehicle in the driveway. *Jordan.* Once the brewing started, she hustled down the hall. Fifteen minutes later with wet hair and older cutoff jeans and a T-shirt, Callie filled two travel mugs before heading to the garage. She rounded the open door and stopped. Jordan was bent over the blueprints, her hair roughly dried, her biceps bulging as she leaned on the table. Admitting she'd been attracted to her from the start was easy, but confessing she was even more so now was harder.

Jordan had taken care of her last night when she couldn't do so for herself. It had been sweet and the kind of attention she didn't often have, but she wasn't about to get used to it. She was out to establish her independence from her family's money and that meant relying on her own resources, both financial and emotional, to get through, not to lean on the first person who'd shown any interest, professionally or otherwise. Besides, Jordan gave off mixed signals of fleeting interest and irritation. She was sure her attraction was one-sided.

"Good morning."

Jordan glanced up. Her brow lifted and a half smile formed. "Morning. How are you feeling?"

She made her legs move, her feet take steps, and was pleasantly surprised to be able to walk without shaking. "Good." She handed off a cup and Jordan nodded thanks. "Actually," she said. "I don't remember too much about what happened after leaving the restaurant."

"Hmm." Jordan's smile reached her eyes.

"What?" Just because she'd asked didn't mean she wanted to know how much she didn't remember. Not really.

Jordan cocked her hip against the framed wall. "I didn't think you'd forget letting me know you're a lesbian." She said it with a straight face, but the twinkle in her eyes gave her away.

"Oh, God." She momentarily hid behind her hand.

"No need to fret, unless it was just a throwaway comment, and it isn't true."

Heat suffused her cheeks. Callie wasn't upset she'd told Jordan about her preference for women, but the "how" would likely be embarrassing. "No, it wasn't but..." There wasn't any easy way to find out. "How'd we get on the topic?"

Jordan looked up. "Let's see. I carried you into the bedroom, sat you on the bed, then removed your shoes. When I suggested you lie down, you patted the bed and said, 'I'm a lesbian. Want to join me?'"

"I did not." Her hand flew to her throat. She fingered the necklace that always rested against her skin, needing to keep her hands busy and her concentration on Jordan's words, not her luscious-looking mouth.

"It might not be word for word, but it's pretty accurate."

What must she think of me? There was a lot of things she could say, but any excuse would be lame. "And then I passed out?" Jordan put on her tool belt and her pulse jumped to attention.

"Pretty much." A shadow darkened her face. "I'm sorry I looked in the medicine chest for some OTC pills."

Callie hated whatever it was that caused Jordan's pain. "Don't apologize for looking after me. Especially when I was in no shape to do it." Against her better judgment, like blurting out her sexual orientation, she placed her hand on Jordan's arm. "Thank you for making sure I was okay."

Jordan's gaze slowly moved over her, the heat of that look sparked a line of fire along her body. "I didn't mind." She glanced at where her hand rested, then lifted the other to lightly stroke her cheek. "You were cute sound asleep." She shook her head. "You're beautiful all the time."

When Jordan leaned closer, her breath froze. Her mouth was so enticing, her lips full. Just when she thought the distance would close, Jordan backed away.

"Are you up for working today?"

The moment passed with a dull thud, and she silently sighed. "I've dressed for the occasion." She indicated what she considered her less than flattering wardrobe, then waved at the plans still spread on the table. "What's on the to-do list?"

Jordan went over the framing that was left for the store, then explained about the rafters and frowned. "I'm going to have to bring in a couple of guys to help with those, but I can put them together."

"We can't do it?"

"They're going to be pretty heavy, and lifting while climbing a ladder makes it twice as hard." Jordan must have recognized her disappointment. "I don't doubt your enthusiasm, but it's dangerous if you've never lifted something like that into position. Even I've taken a tumble or two."

Callie understood the logic, but it still left her feeling inadequate. "So more of what we did yesterday?" She put enthusiasm in her voice. Working with Jordan was a pleasure, and she was learning a lot. Even if she didn't remember every detail, she had a new appreciation for the tradespeople that built homes. It wasn't an easy job.

"Grab your goggles. We've got a ton of cutting to do." Jordan grinned. "Then you get a lesson with the nail gun."

Not in any of her fantasics had she thought she'd be excited about using power tools, and it had nothing at all to do with her instructor. She'd go with that lie for now, since it seemed to be working for her, but Callie wondered how long it would be until she faced reality.

CHAPTER THIRTEEN

The television rumbled in the background. Jordan held her cell phone; the screen seemed to be taunting her. She'd been avoiding calls and texts from her best friend, Mel, for the last few weeks. At first, she told herself she was too busy, which shouldn't have mattered at all. Then she was just plain tired by the long days and fitful sleep. Now she'd run out of excuses and avoidance wasn't going to work much longer. Sooner or later Mel would hunt her down, corner her, and make her talk about whatever had her retreating from their unbreakable connection.

A plausible excuse sat in the wings, but Jordan wasn't sure she wanted to use it. The last time she had feelings for a woman, she'd gone MIA, and Mel knew her too well to be put off by a flimsy reason neither of them would believe. She let out a breath and pressed Mel's contact number.

"You're alive. I'll be damned." Mel's voice held an abundance of sarcasm and rightly so.

She glanced at the flashing images on the TV, not really seeing them. "It's not my first time confessing I suck as a friend."

"True that." Mel went silent long enough for her to prepare for the inevitable. "You already know I'm going to ask who she is, right?"

Jordan slid her hand over her face. "Yeah. I met her on a jobsite. She's a stained-glass artist."

"Not what I expected, but go on."

She started at the beginning and brought Mel up to the point of agreeing to help Callie remodel the garage. By that time, she was reclining and staring at the ceiling, wondering how she'd gotten to the point of wanting more than the only life she knew, the only life she'd allowed herself, until now.

"I want to know one more thing. Is she beautiful?"

"Beyond words." It came out so naturally, and so resolutely, she sat up too quickly, making her head spin.

"Wow." Mel was rarely speechless, and she wondered what would follow. "So when do I meet her?"

"Slow down. We haven't even…I mean, Jesus, we don't even know each other that well." Sure, they'd had a few conversations, but neither of them had revealed much in the way of details. Actually, that wasn't entirely true. She knew far more about Callie than Callie knew about her, and that was totally by design. Jordan didn't want to have the conversations that would let someone into her broken heart or know of the relationship she should have steered clear of, or the utter feelings of ultimate failure and defeat she struggled against on a daily basis.

"And you're falling for her, nonetheless. Not that I'm sad someone besides a quick romp has caught your attention, but I know you. Don't run with your tail between your legs. Be patient and see where things lead."

Mel was right. She chuckled to herself. Mel was usually right about all manner of things they talked about. "You know me too well sometimes." She went to the kitchen and fixed a cup of coffee. A month of catching up lay ahead of her and Mel deserved her full attention.

An hour later Jordan lay in bed, her eyes closed and her heart a bit more open. They set a date for dinner the following week and shooting pool afterward at the Frog, a local bar that in the past had been lesbian only, but now catered to the eclectic mix that summer vacationers offered. She didn't mind sharing space with the rest of humanity, as long as everyone respected each other. Jordan took a minute and thought about Callie setting down roots here, of all places. She knew better than to think it was destiny that landed her in the same town, but to have her on one of Jordan's jobsites was a bit more than coincidence, if you believed in those kinds of things. Skeptical could be her middle name in most instances, but this time there was a nagging pull on her soul that refused to go away. Maybe she didn't want it to. Too many good things had disappeared from her life already. Perhaps it was time to try a different tactic.

The next morning as Jordan stood looking out her kitchen window, she reviewed the day ahead. She had the Callie house, as she'd come to think of it, to wrap up and then let her know she could install the pendant shades over the counter. The last of her tradespeople should be done today, but she'd check the house tomorrow to be sure. Then there was the bid she wanted to submit. The job would keep her and the crew busy for at least two, maybe three months over the winter. She glanced at her buzzing phone and swiped to open the screen, then groaned. She'd sent a card for her mother's birthday like she did every year, however, when she thought about their nonexistent relationship, her gut tightened.

Knowing her mother had a closer relationship with her brothers didn't bother her. But when it came to her father, Jordan hadn't been tolerant at all as to how her mother had let her father's depression progress to the point of suicide. Of course, she hadn't been very observant either, and every day she thought about how absent she'd been in her family's life. That wasn't how she'd been raised.

Jordan picked up the phone with her finger poised just as it stopped, giving her a bit of respite before her conscience kicked in. She went to her contacts and was about to swipe the call button when it rang, startling her. "Fuck." She pressed the handset icon. "Jordan Spade." A few minutes later, she hung up. One of her jobs had a waterline break and immediate decisions had to be made. Maybe she could talk to her mom later. She typed out a quick birthday message and breathed out a sigh of relief. The reprieve was welcome, even though it was temporary. It was past time she tried to reconnect on more than a casual level with her mom. Casual wasn't cutting it for her anymore, and that little nugget was made apparent by her growing fondness for Callie and a shy glance at what the future might hold.

❖

"So, when do we get to visit?" Callie's mom asked.

She looked out the window at the small dumpster that had been delivered yesterday, then thought about the guest room chucked full of her art supplies. "Not until after the renovations are done, Mom. The place is a mess and there's nowhere for you and Dad to sleep." Her mother had been begging to visit even though Callie knew it would turn into a battle of wills like it predictably had in a lot of other instances. Her father, the quieter parent, had told her to take her time settling in. How such opposite personalities had ever come together still baffled her at times. But when it came to social statuses and keeping up with the Joneses, her father was always the first out of the gate. He was just more sensitive to her need to establish her own identity, even if he didn't understand why.

"It will be winter soon, you know." Her mother hated traveling north in winter, or anywhere it was less than eighty degrees. "Are you freezing up there?"

Callie rolled her eyes. "It's not the arctic, Mom. It's been absolutely beautiful." The temperate weather, even in the dead of winter, was one reason she'd picked this location. Florida had two seasons: hot as hell or wet with the constant threat of hurricanes. When she was a preteen, and then later a teenager, the lure of the beach had lost its appeal when she discovered there were only a couple of months out of the year that she could actually enjoy it. And the nonstop need to be in air conditioning and closed up inside for weeks at a time made her claustrophobic. The night she and Jordan had strolled along the bustling streets on the way to dinner had been wonderful. Her mother's voice jarred her out of the memory.

"Well, I suppose as long as there's no snow a trip would be doable."

Her mother's glider was the only background sound. Unlike when she sat on her porch and a symphony of life greeted her. Birds sang in the nearby trees. Distant waves crashed on the beach. Crickets and cicadas played music. The faraway drone of the voices of visitors and residents alike that included peals of laughter gave her a sense of belonging. Rehoboth was full of life and she never felt alone, and although occasionally she recognized her loneliness, it wasn't something she chose to dwell on.

"Thanksgiving would be a nice time, don't you think?" her mother asked.

There's no way to get out of a visit. "It'll be close, but I think the garage will be done by then. Why don't you and Dad talk it over? You could fly up for a long weekend."

"Just a weekend?" The tone of the question was one her mother used when she expected Callie to give in.

"Arrive on Wednesday and head home on Sunday. It'll be a nice visit." *And not too long for anyone, including me.* "There's a lot of Tanger outlets. We could spend a whole day updating your wardrobe." She was going for the jugular, and that suited her fine.

"Really?" Her mother's silence meant she was thinking. "I suppose your father could manage a few days without becoming frustrated. The pictures you sent looked inviting. But I'm not walking the beach when it's cold."

"Talk to Dad first. You know he hates when you make plans without him."

"I know, dear, he's just not good at that sort of thing, but I promise we'll talk. Love you."

"Love you, too, Mom."

In a little more than two months she would have to batten down the hatches and prepare Rehoboth for the monsoon that was her mother. Blowing in on a gust of wind and sucking the air out when she left. Although, for all the angst they created in her life with their disappointed looks and off-key remarks, she missed her parents. It would be good to see them, especially if the visit included a foursome.

CHAPTER FOURTEEN

The bone-crushing hug from Mel helped to remind Jordan how much she missed seeing her. Totally on her, the avoidance tactic was all hers too. She'd used it so many times in her life it had become second nature. At one point Jordan thought she had a handle on it. Clearly, she was wrong.

"You're a sight." Mel sat on a stool and turned to face her. "I'm going to grill you, but not until we've had a drink and I've gotten another update."

They ordered whiskey sours, giving her a clue how the conversation was going to go. There'd be no stalling. She might be able to get away with it on the phone, but not in person. She held up her glass and Mel did the same. "Truth."

"Truth," Mel said, repeating their years-old salute to their friendship. "Details."

The shorthand communication between them had developed out of necessity. They'd worked together a long time ago at a factory and the machines that ran in the background constantly drowned out most conversations. When they did stop, they'd rush to get in a word or two, then smiled when they figured it out, and waited for the next moment of silence. It had been a fun time in both their lives when they were young and carefree and woman crazy. When Jordan let go of the hard-won control she fought to maintain these days, she felt that way again. At one time she hoped those carefree days weren't going to be only sporadic moments, but rather the way she lived her life. That day simply had to come along soon, and she was counting on Mel being there when it did.

"Callie showed up on the jobsite off Holland Glade Road. I found her in the kitchen taking measurements."

"So you said last week. Quit stalling."

Jordan laughed. She considered what had taken place in the last few days. "Callie's been a great assistant. She's learning a lot about framing and drywall."

"You're playing teacher?" When she nodded Mel went on. "And she hasn't tried to kill you yet? That's an accomplishment for sure."

"Hey, I'm a good instructor."

"I'm sure you were your charming self." Mel's brow rose in the telltale sign she knew Jordan had been anything but charming.

"Very funny. You know how I run my sites, and for good reason I might add." A few years back a nosy neighbor took it upon himself to check out a house she was building. He never should have gone inside, but no one had seen him enter. The next thing she knew he was screaming for help after he'd tripped over the fireplace hearth and taken a nasty fall. Lucky for everyone, he knew the owners, and after a number of stitches and some well-timed jokes, the owners had assured her neither party was going to press charges.

"Hey, I get that, but you said she's beautiful so your mind should be on that instead of bossing her around."

She *had* been bullish at the beginning, along with annoyed. It was a wonder Callie hadn't written her off from the start. "Yeah, well, you already know what a charmer I am." She smiled. Mel studied her in that contemplative way she had. She always thought before she spoke. She went on to tell her about her lesbian confession. She wasn't sure if she regretted sharing that because she didn't want Mel to make fun of Callie, or if she felt it was a betrayal by sharing something that probably should have stayed between her and Callie.

"Tell you what we're going to do." She gestured to the bartender for another round. "We'll move to a table, order a pizza, and I'm going to make you realize how much of an ass you are for not having at least kissed this woman."

The laughter that bubbled up from her depths felt like a breath of fresh air. She'd been tense since she'd begun working with Callie. Not that she wasn't enjoying being a teacher of sorts, but the attraction was both uplifting and distracting, and the rollercoaster of emotions had set her on edge more than once. As they settled into a booth, the image of feeling Callie's lips beneath hers brought a swift, undeniable physical response. She was in trouble, and she knew it.

❖

Callie carefully surveyed the fruit. It was a tantalizing kaleidoscope of eye-catching color, presented in a tastefully arranged display. She glanced at the other shoppers who were dressed in casual attire, the colors mimicking the contents of the bins in front of her. Most chatted and laughed. Some greeting each other with a sense of familiarity. None gave her the impression they were runway models on display with their noses in the air like in the elite section of Florida. This atmosphere suited her much better. Maybe she was becoming stodgy, but she didn't think a grocery store was any place to show off the latest high-end fashions while snubbing noses at those who either didn't go for that kind of indulgence or couldn't afford them. Her mother was a prime example of uppity and she hated how much she'd acted like her until she became immersed in the world of art where being different or non-conforming to societal expectations was applauded. She was especially glad she didn't see any men in Speedos. No one needed to be exposed to that kind of show. Eww. She picked up a cantaloupe and listened for the hollow sound as she tapped her knuckle on the skin, then pushed on the stem depression.

"If it talks back, I'm out of here."

The deep, gravelly voice close to her ear made her jump. "Jesus." Callie's heart raced. It was only from being startled and not because of the person who owned the voice. She turned and mock-glared at Jordan who stood next to a cart with a look of utter amusement on her face.

"Are you stalking me?" A sliver of excitement shot through Callie.

"Nope, sorry. Giant's having a price war with the competition and there's a few bargains I wanted to get in on before they sold out." Jordan jutted her chin toward the cantaloupe in Callie's hand. "So what's the word from the fruit?"

"Hmph. Don't be a naysayer. It's the best way to tell if it will be sweet and juicy." She put it in her cart. When she turned around to find Jordan watching her she caught her bottom lip in her teeth and waited. She was being more forward than normal, but Jordan didn't seem to mind as she picked out a melon and held it out in her large hand.

"Share your secret?" Jordan's mouth quirked in a sexy, one-sided grin.

Undaunted by her skepticism, Callie took the melon and rolled one palm under it, then poised her bent knuckle near the depression. "You want to hear a hollow sound, then double check by pressing the dimple. If it gives, it's ripe. The tapping works better with watermelon, but I use both methods for cantaloupe because the skin is thicker." She demonstrated her technique. The sound was dull, and the dimple didn't budge. "Try another. This one's not ripe."

Jordan's brow rose as she took it back and picked another before presenting it.

"You try, then I'll let you know if I agree." She couldn't believe she was fondling fruit with Jordan, but any reason to spend time with her worked for Callie. She'd examine what that said about her head space later.

Jordan mimicked the ritual. "Not sure about the sound, but this," she pointed to the depression, "is soft."

Callie went through the tap and press, then agreed. It was just shy of being fully ripe. "Are you going to eat it today?"

"Probably not for a day or two. I have a couple of bananas that need rescuing before they're beyond edible."

She set the melon in Jordan's cart. "Should be good by then."

"Thanks for the lesson." Jordan lingered, watching her. Waiting.

What the hell. "I'm grilling tonight if you don't have plans. Nothing too exciting. Just burgers and macaroni salad. If you're not in a rush, we could watch a movie after." She'd almost said, "or something" but scaled back her enthusiasm at the last minute. She really had to rein in her wayward thoughts.

"Thanks for the invitation. I'll accept on one condition."

Callie moved her hand to her cocked hip. "And what would that be?"

"I bring the salad and beer."

"Should I be leery? This is the first I've heard that you actually prepare food."

Jordan's rich, deep laughter rang through the air, and she liked the sound.

"I hate cooking for one, but I like to cook. No one's flopped down dead yet from anything I've made. So what do you say?"

It was a terrible idea. She should have never invited her. Getting close to Jordan sent off all kinds of warning bells because a woman in her life could derail her priorities, but only if she let her, and Callie was in total control where Jordan was concerned. "Okay." A low current ran through her body, and she knew exactly why she'd extended the invitation. Callie glanced at her phone. "How does six sound?"

"Sounds like a plan to me." Jordan began to turn, then faced her again. "You allergic to anything?"

"Not that I'm aware of."

"See you later then." Jordan strode off toward the vegetables.

When she realized she was still staring, she whipped her cart around. The bin of "mini me" watermelons loomed in front of her. Grilled watermelon would round out the meal and might be something Jordan hadn't had before. She liked providing new experiences for her. Jordan making something for her was a bonus. One she was looking forward to a little more than she probably should.

❖

Aside from some meager and altogether simple dinners consisting of a protein and an occasional vegetable, Jordan hadn't really done any cooking to speak of in her remodeled kitchen. The tattered recipe book she'd gotten from her mother when she was in high school, along with a note that said if she "ever expected to land a husband, she ought to know how to cook," was one of the most laughable things her mother had given her. Her mom wasn't big on hugs or affection, and Jordan had felt much the same about her. Theirs had never been a typical mother/daughter relationship, and likely never would be. Jordan had always been closer to her father, probably because they had much more in common than not. Her brothers might look like him, but that's where their similarities ended.

She rinsed the ditalini in cold water, dumped it into a bowl, and shoved it into the fridge to finish cooling. Meanwhile, she peeled the hard-boiled eggs. She moved around the kitchen with a familiarity that should have felt odd, considering how little time she spent in it, but having someone to share her creation with made a big difference. It gave purpose to what she was doing and that, too, was rare.

Half an hour later, Jordan hit the shower. The thirty minutes before she had to leave was plenty of time to get clean and dressed. She wasn't into trying to impress anyone, but as she stood in her closet deciding what to wear she realized that's exactly what she was doing. With time running out, she grabbed a pair of black jeans and a lightweight gray Henley shirt. The three open buttons made the shirt all the more comfortable by not being close to her throat, something she hated. Jordan ran her hands through her damp hair, turned from the hallway mirror, and gathered the salad and beer. Anticipation beat like the wings of butterflies in her stomach, soft but constant. She didn't get excited about being in the presence of another woman. Jordan enjoyed their company for a few hours before moving on, and though she hadn't even done that in months aside from some meals with Callie, tonight felt different.

She could have said no. Could have lied and told her she'd made other plans. She didn't owe Callie more than common courtesy. Everything about her made Jordan question behaviors that had become rote and uncomplicated. So much so that she discovered denying her growing feelings was foolhardy, and the driving force for constantly saying yes. How many more times would she say yes where Callie was concerned remained to be determined. Jordan smiled as she walked out the door.

CHAPTER FIFTEEN

"Hi," Callie said when she greeted Jordan at the door. Jordan stepped over the threshold and smiled.

"Hello. I come bearing essentials." She held up a covered glass bowl and a four-pack of beer.

She took the bowl. "Refrigerator?"

Jordan followed her to the kitchen. "Unless we're going to eat soon, that would be best." Jordan set the beer on the counter. "I hope you like stout."

"I like most stouts, especially with beef." She read the label on the carrier. "Dragon's Milk?"

Jordan laughed. "Yeah. This is a treat. It's aged in bourbon barrels and has a high alcohol content. This one has ten percent, but they make an eleven and a twelve. Three is my absolute limit. Two over several hours is usually enough."

"I did so well the last time we drank, I'm surprised you're giving me another chance." She laughed and Jordan chuckled.

"Being at home has its advantages. I'm sure you'll be fine." Jordan shoved her hand into her pocket and looked anywhere but at Callie.

"Should we have one now? I haven't started the grill, and the burgers need to come to room temp before I cook them."

"Sure. Yeah." Jordan looked grateful to have something to do. Once she had the bottles open, she pushed the remainders forward.

"They should go in the freezer. This is best ice cold." She held up the open ones.

"How about we sit on the front porch and soak up the last of the sun?" She didn't mind that fall was making its appearance because it was her favorite time of the year. The autumn colors hadn't started yet, and she wondered when they'd begin. She held the door open, and Jordan stepped out, then sat on one of the cushy chairs she'd found at a garage sale. She looked across the short distance separating them and caught Jordan's gaze. "Is this okay?" Her house was situated on a less traveled street, but the area was full of seasonal rentals and people strolled by at a leisurely pace.

"It's perfect." Jordan held out a bottle and picked up her own. "To sunsets by the ocean."

"I'll definitely drink to that." The bottle was very cold, and she wondered if Jordan had stored them in her own freezer for a time. After a tentative sip, she let the brew sit on her tongue before swallowing. The taste held notes of coffee and chocolate with a very smooth finish, nothing like the other stouts she'd had. "This is really good."

"Glad you like it. It's my favorite. For obvious reasons, I only have it once in a while." Jordan took another swig before setting the bottle on the small table next to her.

The more she was around her, the more Callie wanted to know about her. "How did you end up being a general contractor?" The shadow that showed every now and again reappeared and eclipsed the light from Jordan's eyes. "I'm sorry. Don't answer that. I'm just being nosy." She regretted treading on an obvious sore spot for Jordan, but she didn't know how to avoid them if she didn't know what had caused them.

Jordan took another drink and held the bottle on her thigh. "It's fine." She took a deep breath, held it, then let it out slowly. "My father was a mason. My brother and I followed in his footsteps. When he…" Jordan swallowed before continuing. "After he died it felt too close to all the raw emotions to continue doing what he loved. I knew some people I could ask about teaching me how to be a contractor. I spent a year as an apprentice until I learned what I needed to know and was confident I could do it on my own. That's when JS, General Contractor was born."

"How long has JS been in business?"

"Five years, give or take. Some of the time is a bit fuzzy." Jordan looked directly into her eyes. "I wasn't in a good place at the beginning, but I'm better now."

Ignoring the warning that droned through her brain, Callie took Jordan's hand and squeezed. "From everything I've seen, you're doing fine."

Jordan squeezed back, then slipped her hand away. "What do you think about the progress?" Jordan tipped her head toward the garage.

"It's great. I'm not sure if I'm actually helping or in the way. I hope you'll be honest with me about that. I don't want to slow you down."

"You haven't. I'm impressed you've picked up as much as you have." Jordan set her nearly empty bottle down. "Have you given any thought to creating a piece of your work for the shop itself?"

Callie immersed herself in the liquid honey color of Jordan's eyes as they flowed over her, warming her skin. In the last few weeks, she'd seen less of her gruff side and more of a gentler nature surface and couldn't help wondering which was the real Jordan. Maybe it depended on whether Jordan needed a barrier to keep people at a distance, or that she didn't want others to see she had a soft underbelly. Either way, the only one Callie was interested in was the honest one. She had a feeling Jordan had grown so used to hiding that side of herself, maybe even she didn't know which was real anymore.

"Every time I think I've come up with something I change my mind." She finished her beer and picked up Jordan's empty. When she stood the world momentarily tilted until strong hands steadied her.

"Whoa there. You okay?" Jordan's warm breath tickled along her neck.

She took a minute to get her bearings. "You weren't lying when you said the beer had a kick." After a deep breath, her vision came back into focus. "I'm good." Jordan's hands fell from her hips, and she suppressed the groan that almost broke free. "I think we should get dinner started."

"Great idea," Jordan said and followed her inside.

She set the bottles next to the sink, pulled a water out of the fridge, and downed half. "Want one?"

"Might water down my buzz, but I suppose I should." She took the bottle, cracked the seal, and drank it down in one fluid gulp while her throat moved rhythmically as she swallowed.

Callie continued to stare, unable to move. Unable to do anything but watch Jordan's every move.

"Do you want me to start the grill?"

She shook her head free of the lust that had gathered. "Yes. Thank you. Everything you need should be out there."

"I'll try not to burn the house down." Jordan grinned.

Alone, she held on to the counter. What the hell? She needed to get a grip. Jordan was her guest and one beer in, she was making a total fool of herself. Again. Jesus. She could only imagine what Jordan must think of her. She pulled the container of sliced watermelon from the fridge and set it on the tray along with salt and pepper. Fresh ciabatta rolls sat in a covered basket. A jar of sandwich pickles was on the counter. The whoosh of the screen made her pulse race, pulling her from her attempt to settle her nerves by listing the things around her.

"Grill's nice and hot. Would you like me to carry that out?" Jordan pointed to the tray. It wasn't heavy, but with her equilibrium less than one hundred percent, she didn't want to chance dumping their dinner.

"Would probably be safer for the food if you did."

Jordan shrugged. "No worries."

Callie pulled the screen open, and Jordan brushed by with the tray, her forearm grazing her enough to send a shockwave through her.

"Do you want me to grill? I don't mind." Jordan's sincerity was touching.

This was the Jordan she wanted to know more about. Who had formed her? What darkened her mood and turned her somber? Why the hell was someone this capable, accomplished, and hot still single? Not that she was complaining. "Thanks, but I invited you. I'm better now." She seasoned the burgers, adjusted the flame, and put them on the grill. "Do you want cheese? I have a sharp cheddar or pepper jack."

"Hard decision." Jordan leaned against the railing, hands braced on either side of her hips. The muscles in her thighs bulged against the jean material. Her ankles crossed in a casual, relaxed way. "Sharp is good."

Callie's gaze slowly moved up along her body until she met Jordan's eyes staring back at her. Heat reflected in them, and desire coursed through her. When Jordan licked her lips, the fire inside flared.

"You might want to check the burgers."

She was having a hard time concentrating. "What?" Jordan pointed behind her. Smoke billowed out of the grill. "Shit." Flames shot up and the sizzle of searing meat met her as she raised the top. It was a minor miracle that the burgers, sporting perfect grill marks, weren't charred black. She flipped them and moved them around, then lowered the lid. "They survived." Callie hoped her smile helped cover her embarrassment.

"It's grilling. I don't mind a little char."

"You're sweet." Ugh. Another uncensored remark. At this rate she was going to make a total fool of herself. "I'm going to get the cheese. Do you mind keeping an eye on them?"

"It would be my pleasure."

Jordan went to the grill, and she went inside for the cheese and a clean platter. She hadn't gotten around to buying an outdoor table to eat on yet, but with fall at the doorstep and winter just a few months away, spring would be time enough.

"How are they looking?"

Flipping the burgers with a flick of her wrist, Jordan grinned over her shoulder. "Like they want to be eaten."

Callie's brow shot up as if it had a mind of her own and Jordan's cheeks colored. "Well, in that case the cheese is up." Jordan stepped aside and she placed a slice on each. She opened the container and placed six slices of melon on the grill, turning the flame low.

"Grilled melon, huh?" Jordan peeked over her shoulder. "So you were looking for a victim today?"

She turned and looked up at Jordan. The features of her handsome face stood in stark relief against the lowering sun, the shallow crow's feet lending to her attractiveness. If she moved a few inches, their lips would meet. "We'll have to eat inside. I haven't gotten around to buying a table."

"I could make you one."

"That's not necessary." The ongoing argument in her head about why kissing Jordan would complicate her life and take precedent over her desire for making art her life, not just "a pastime" as her mother so eloquently called it. As valid as that sounded, her libido was all in.

"Unless you'd rather have something other than wood, I don't mind. It will give me a project to look forward to when work is slow in the winter."

Callie flipped the melon and moved the burgers from the flame. "I'm not sure if any other material would hold up as well under the salt air. Wood is perfect." One more thing she'd have to show her appreciation for. The quick flash of a bedroom scene with Jordan on her back made her gasp. Luckily, she'd turned from Jordan, and in the time it took to move everything onto the platter she was able to back away from the visceral image. "Ready to dig in?"

"More than ready." Jordan's muscles flexed as she reached for the tray. "Not that you need help."

Smiling, she acquiesced and opened the door.

"Where do you want this?"

"On the table. I'll get dishes." Nope. Not going to fixate on Jordan's muscular body or the look in her eyes. She stretched to an upper cabinet to pull out two plates, but her palms were a bit sweaty, and they immediately began to slip from her grasp. Hands shot over her to catch them and a warm body pressed into her, pinning her against the lower cabinet. Jordan set the plates down, caught her shoulders, and gently turned her.

"Are you all right?"

Her chest rose and fell rapidly. Jordan was still too close, and heat radiated from her body. If she didn't move away, she wasn't sure what she'd do. And just like that, Jordan's lips pressed to hers in the kind of kiss she'd been waiting for since they'd met. The soft, gentle caress was like none she'd ever had. Before she could fully grasp what was happening, they were gone.

Jordan took a half step back while continuing to hold Callie. "I'm not going to tell you I'm sorry, because I'm not." She brushed her thumb across Callie's lower lip. "Unless you want to throw out the food, we should probably eat."

Callie blinked several times as though trying to comprehend what had happened.

Jordan wasn't sure she knew either. She'd gone with her gut, which was an oddity since she usually overanalyzed everything in her life. "Burgers, salad, grilled watermelon?"

Callie's eyes snapped into focus. "Right. Dinner." She went for the cabinet.

"The plates are here. What else?"

Callie pulled open a drawer so quickly the silverware inside rattled loudly. She looked proud when she produced utensils for two, a serving spoon, and set of tongs. "These," she said as she spun before grabbing a stack of napkins from the wooden holder. Jordan followed with the plates and her salad.

"Do you want your other beer?"

"Definitely." Callie said it with a straight face and Jordan turned away so she wouldn't see her smile.

She set an open bottle by Callie's plate and sat across from her. When Callie reached for the basket of rolls, she caught her hand. "Thank you for the invitation."

"You're welcome." Callie glanced between their joined hands and Jordan. She visibly swallowed.

Jordan let go. "And for the kiss."

Callie dropped the spoon she'd used to scoop salad back in the bowl. "About that. You can't just body slam a woman, then kiss her." She took a pull of beer and sat back, looking anywhere but at her.

She was one foot in and the decision to go all the way loomed. "Why not?"

Callie's head whipped up so fast Jordan thought she might have injured herself. Clearly needing something to do with her hands, she attacked her burger like it had offended her in some way. "Because it's…" She stabbed a piece of watermelon and bit down, the juice running down her chin. Unbothered by the pale pink liquid trail, Callie took another bite.

Jordan wanted to lick every bit from Callie's lips, imagining the mix of sweet and salt on her tongue. After taking a steadying breath, she pressed for more. "Because it's what?"

"You're going to make me say it, aren't you?"

Jordan fought against smiling. "Yes."

Callie's lips pursed. "You can't if my mouth is full." She picked up the thick burger she'd shoved into a roll after spreading mayo and ketchup on it and took a huge bite, filling her mouth.

Laughter exploded from Jordan. Between difficult looking chews, Callie joined in when she could without choking. Jordan forced a serious look that she didn't feel. "If you choke I'll have to kiss you again. I'll make sure you're breathing first, but I'm going with it." Jordan tried for nonchalance as she fixed her burger. "Is that what you want?" She glanced up and met Callie's vivid green eyes staring at her. She'd wiped away the trail of juice and Jordan mourned its absence.

"I don't think that's a good idea. We didn't start off on the best of terms and we managed to move on. I wouldn't want to jeopardize our friendship." Callie glanced away.

"Do you think it would?"

Callie took a smaller bite, concentration clearly written on her face. "I've never had a serious relationship." She took a drink and wiped the condiment overflow from her face. It was adorable. "I mean, I've done short-term, convenient arrangements. I was really busy in college and then I dove into the world of art."

Jordan didn't miss the gleam in Callie's eyes when the word *art* flowed from her soft, glistening lips. "You never wanted a deeper connection with anyone?" She'd tried to find some sense of belonging with her ex, Shelley, even though she ended up being the wrong person. She sensed sadness from Callie and her chest tightened.

"I put all my energy into my goals, except for occasional, much-needed sex." Callie flashed a grin, but even that seemed forced. "I had to keep my focus where it belonged, not on the fantasy world in my head." Callie shrugged and pushed her near empty plate to the side before meeting her gaze. "I'm not ready for more. I still have things to achieve."

Something sharp twisted in her gut. She hadn't thought it through before kissing Callie. She hadn't been thinking at all. She'd simply acted, and the kiss hadn't disappointed. All she'd been thinking about since arriving was how beautiful Callie was and how enticing her lips looked. Then when the opportunity presented itself, she hadn't hesitated, she'd simply gone with the desire coursing through her. Now she had to figure out how to salvage the night and whatever this was between them. She'd been sure Callie's glances held hers a little too long, sure she was having similar feelings, but she'd been wrong before. "You're right. We have a project to complete." After a few silent beats, she added, "I didn't mean to make the situation awkward. I'm sorry." She bit into her burger, slowly chewed, and swallowed the regret of one more mistake she'd made. Callie wasn't interested in anything more than getting the garage done, and the other night had been fueled by alcohol, nothing more. At least now she knew where they stood. It didn't change the fact she still wished things were different.

❖

The TV flashed in front of Callie in the dimly lit room. Jordan wasn't really there. Since the clean-up of dinner and her brilliant reasoning as to why getting involved would be a bad idea she wanted to dig a deep hole and jump in. The fear of pushing her business to the back burner in lieu of a relationship that might not even work made her back off. Like she had for a year in Florida before she realized her family's influence had continued to make her second-guess herself about choosing art over teaching. Jordan wasn't like them at all. And when she had presented the perfect opportunity to further things, Callie had shot her down. *What an idiot.* She glanced across the gulf between them and took a breath for courage.

"Jordan?"

Jordan was slow to respond, looking as though the movie playing was the most riveting thing in the room. Callie would have told her how wrong she was. Jordan was the most interesting and eye-catching woman she'd ever met, and she wanted Jordan to know that.

"Hmm?" Jordan slowly faced her.

"I didn't really mean it when I said it was a bad idea. I like you."

"That's good because I like you, too." She turned sideways and moved a bit closer. "About the kiss—"

"Please don't tell me you regret it." Against her better judgment…well, her skewed judgment when it came to Jordan, Callie didn't want to think it hadn't affected Jordan like it had her.

"I was going to say, the moment was perfect and so was the kiss."

Warmth spread through her as she remembered Jordan's lips pressed to hers. She wouldn't mind a repeat, but now didn't seem to be the time. "It was amazing." Callie watched as Jordan's honey eyes darkened, glimpses of desire swirling in their depths. She wanted to be the focus of that desire, no matter what she'd *said*, what she was feeling was the opposite, but that voice in her head could still be heard. "I need to go slow for now. There's been a lot happening."

"Glad that's settled then." Jordan smiled before turning back to the TV. "What are we watching?"

Callie chuckled. "I'm not sure either, but it's supposed to be funny."

Jordan reached for the remote. "Shall we start it over so we have a clue what's going on?"

She waved her assent. "Be my guest." She was going to say Jordan had the power, but she wasn't interested in a one-sided relationship. Jordan restarted the movie then moved close enough that they could touch if either of them ventured to do so. That was part of the problem. Callie wanted more of Jordan in so many ways her head spun. She really needed to get a grip on her runaway libido, but Jordan's androgynous good looks made it nearly impossible. "Would you like coffee with dessert?" Having something to do other than stare at Jordan's profile would redirect her attention, if only for a short time.

"Dessert? Coffee? Who could turn that down?" Jordan's bright smile was like a beacon. "Can I help?"

Callie shook her head. "Just get me up to speed on the movie when I return. No need to pause it." She needed the space. Needed to rationalize what she was doing with Jordan when her mind and her body were in constant conflict. Not that there was anything wrong with what she was doing. She was a grown woman and being attracted to someone wasn't a bad thing. Right? But there was so much about Jordan she didn't know, like what caused her to become sullen or her temper to flare. She had a feeling it had something to do with her father, but that might not be true. Until she knew for sure it was all speculation on her part, and she didn't want to base decisions about her future on anything but facts. Jordan deserved that much from her.

She filled the pitcher with cream, placed sugar and two mugs on the tray, along with a plate of shortbread cookies, then carried it into the living room to find Jordan smiling at the TV. "What's happening?"

Jordan quickly made room on the coffee table and gave a short synopsis. "Those look delicious." She licked her lips.

"Glad you approve. I never know if I should just stick with lemon cake because people either love it or hate it. There's no in-between. But then I saw this recipe and remembered how well shortbread goes with everything." She filled Jordan's mug and watched as she added cream. "Hmm."

"What?" Jordan glanced between the mug, Callie, and the creamer she still held.

"I could have sworn you put sugar in your coffee."

"Oh." Jordan waved her hand. "Sometimes I do, sometimes not. Usually not when there's dessert." She winked and Callie's heartbeat quickened.

"What's your favorite dessert?"

"Anything homemade is best. I don't really have a favorite, though I do love a good fruit pie."

"Apple?" It had been a while since she'd done anything that creative in the kitchen. For Jordan she'd make an exception.

"Not really. I know it's the most popular, but I like peach or cherry best. Blueberry's right up there, too."

Callie stored the information for a later time. Maybe they'd have more dinners together. She could offer to bring dessert and surprise her one night. "That's funny because I don't like apple that much either, unless it's a Dutch caramel crumb top version."

Jordan paused with the cookie just inches from her mouth. "That sounds like something I'd try." Jordan's lips closed over it.

When she bit down, she moaned, and Callie's center tightened. "This is so good." She took another bite. Her tongue appeared and swiped at the crumbs clinging to her lips. She reached for another but drank from her mug instead. "I'm going to slow down to savor every morsel."

Callie couldn't help being pleased by Jordan's reaction. "I'll send you home with some. I can't possibly eat a whole batch, nor should I." They ate in relative silence as the movie played on in the background. She abandoned trying to keep up with what was going on. Jordan was much more interesting than a movie filled with people she didn't know and had no desire to get close to. Was that what she wanted with Jordan? To get closer? Could she control her natural urge for a physical connection while focusing on building her business?

After finishing off a third cookie, Jordan smacked her lips, and grinned ear to ear. "They were delicious." She sipped from her mug while her eyes never wavered from Callie's.

"Are we working on the garage tomorrow?"

Jordan set her empty mug down. She raised the carafe, but Jordan declined more. "I have two jobsites to check on, so it will be later. Ten or eleven before I get here, barring anything that delays me. Do you want me to text or call first?"

"I've got a few errands to run tomorrow myself. If I'm not here start without me, and I'll join you when I get home."

She glanced at the TV and was surprised to see the credits rolling. Where had the time gone? Jordan scooted toward the edge of the couch.

"I should get going." She picked up her napkin and mug.

Callie didn't want the night to end. She hadn't thought about anything physical happening between her and Jordan when she'd extended the invitation, but she couldn't get the kiss out of her mind. The idea that Jordan's mouth could possibly bring other pleasures to her neglected body certainly made for some of what she was feeling. She pulled out a container, placed half the cookies in it, and set it in front of where Jordan stood. "For whenever you want to make those moans again." Oh, God. Had she actually said that out loud?

Jordan chuckled. "My tastebuds will appreciate it." She took a step forward, glanced between Callie's eyes and her lips. "Thank you for a wonderful evening." Her fingers brushed down Callie's arm and caught her hand. "Walk me out?"

All she could do was nod. Jordan seemed as reluctant as she was to end their evening. Standing by the door felt more like a punishment than a simple good-bye. She was about to tell Jordan not to go when Jordan set the container on the small table by the door, then slid her hands up Callie's arms and held her. "I want to kiss you, but only if you want to."

She swallowed the nervous knot. "Why are you asking?"

"Because you said I can't just kiss you without warning." She took a step closer until only the barest space separated them. "But that doesn't mean I'm not going to kiss you because I really have to."

Callie lost herself in the moment when Jordan bent to her waiting mouth. This time the kiss wasn't as gentle as the first. Not rough, but…possessive…and she wanted more. More kisses, more touches, more time with Jordan. Their introduction may have started on the wrong foot, but their newfound friendship was blossoming into so much more, and she needed to rein in her emotions, if even for a little while because it wasn't all about her. Jordan had issues. Who didn't, really? But whatever eclipsed her internal light wasn't something to be overlooked. The impulsive young girl she used to be had grown up to realize if she wasn't careful, if she didn't take her time to see the bigger picture, things could go sideways and throw her off track. Like mistaking wealth for happiness and having it easy, when what she should focus on was working hard to get what she wanted. For now Callie pushed the internal wariness away as she sank deeper into the sensation of Jordan holding her, and her tongue playing over her lips. She was about to let her in when Jordan gently backed away.

"You make me want things I haven't wanted in a very long time." Jordan's hand shook as it traveled downward until they were no longer touching.

"What things? And why so long?" She couldn't imagine why Jordan didn't have a girlfriend. *Oh my God.* Did she have a girlfriend? Callie hadn't even bothered to ask. Maybe that was the shadow. Maybe it was guilt that Jordan was dealing with. Shit, shit. Jordan tapped her forehead.

"What are you thinking?" Jordan brushed some stray hairs away from her face. "Whatever it is, it must be a doozie."

She chewed her bottom lip, knowing she had to ask. "Do you have a girlfriend?"

Jordan laughed bitterly. "Hardly. You don't see them pounding the pavement after me, do you?"

"No. Why is that?"

Jordan shook her head. "Not tonight. I'd rather end this evening on a high note, and kissing you is definitely a high note." In a parting gesture, Jordan's lips brushed over hers once more.

Callie searched for a plausible reason for Jordan to stay. A faulty light switch. A heavy box that needed moving. Her empty bed. "Wait. Your salad."

"Keep it. I'll bring something to go with it tomorrow. We'll have to eat at some point." Jordan opened the door and the balmy, salty air greeted them. "I'll be here before noon. Sleep well, Callie."

The tightness in her chest wasn't anything she was used to experiencing. She hadn't meant to develop an affinity for Jordan. Not really. It happened organically, like the tide slowly inching up the shore. She waved as Jordan backed out of the drive and watched her turn at the end of the street, then she was gone. Callie inhaled deeply. Back inside, she leaned against the door and touched her slightly swollen lips. Tomorrow she'd ask Jordan more about her life, her past. Before she got too involved, she had to know the things Jordan hid. She didn't think it wise when people kept secrets. Her grandmother had given up her dream of pursuing her passion as an artist and kept her broken heart secreted because of her grandparents telling her that her place was helping with the household expenses, not off on some half-cocked fancy of being an artist. Callie was convinced she'd died with the regret that decision brought, and she had promised she wouldn't settle for less than following her dreams, no matter the cost.

She finished cleaning up in the kitchen and turned out the lights. Throughout her nightly routine, all she could think about was the warmth of Jordan's nearness and the press of her lips. When she slipped beneath the covers, she automatically reached for the empty side, and wondered if Jordan would ever be there.

CHAPTER SIXTEEN

By the time Jordan made it to Callie's it was nearly one in the afternoon. Several delayed deliveries kept her on endless calls to track down the missing materials. Then she'd discovered some shoddy work by one of the contractors and had needed a conversation with him to make sure it would be fixed in no uncertain terms. Both had set her behind several hours. Such was her life.

The day had turned warmer than usual for September, and she was glad to see the garage door was open, greeting her like a real homecoming. Callie's car was parked along the side and her pulse picked up tempo. Jordan hadn't been able to get the kisses they'd shared out of her mind. Callie had been caught off guard by the first, and so had Jordan. She'd acted on impulse and the result had only fueled her desire for more. Thinking about how flustered Callie was at the dinner table made her chuckle.

Jordan strapped on her tool belt and began humming a familiar tune, a testament to her upbeat mood. Callie appeared from the house carrying a large cooler with wheels and she rushed to help.

"Let me get that." She was surprised at the weight. "What have you got in here?" She set it on the ground.

Callie shrugged. "I figured you'd been working all morning, so I made lunch."

"Shit." She'd told Callie she'd bring something to have with her leftover salad. "I forgot to get sandwiches. I'll go get them now."

Callie's fingers wrapped around her wrist. "No need. I've got plenty of stuff in there." Callie lightly tapped the cooler with her foot and grabbed the handle. "Let's eat before we start." She smiled and pulled the cooler behind her.

Jordan fell in step beside her. When she reached the doorway, she stopped in her tracks. There was a folding table with a checkered tablecloth and two chairs. A small vase of flowers sat in the middle of two place settings. "Wow."

"It's too nice to not take advantage of a little more of the weather." Callie pulled the cart to a stop and started unpacking. There was last night's salad, a large, wrapped charcuterie board, a basket of bread sticks, crackers, and artisan bread. The last thing she produced was a container of assorted olives. "I'm not sure if we should indulge, but I've got a really nice bottle of pinot grigio, or we can be mindful and have iced tea."

As much as the idea of having a romantic lunch with Callie appealed to her, drinking wasn't smart if they were going to use power tools. "I'd love to, but we should probably skip the alcohol."

Callie nodded and produced two bottles of organic tea. "I wasn't sure if you were going to make it today," she said before setting out serving utensils.

She scooped a little salad onto her plate, then chose a few hunks of cheese. "Delivery issues were the bulk of my morning, then there was some work done on another site that I wasn't happy with, so I had to track down the company's owner and get him to make sure it got fixed." When she glanced up, Callie was watching her intently. "What?"

"You really enjoy what you do."

Heat traveled up her neck and landed in her face. At one time, she thought about getting out of construction altogether, but she couldn't. Like it or not it was in her blood. "I don't know if I enjoy it so much as I think I'm fairly competent at running a jobsite."

She popped a hunk of cheese into her mouth. As she chewed she considered what she liked about the work she did. "I guess I like organizing all the moving parts. Coordinating the craftspeople and making sure things are done in an order that makes sense."

"I could tell that about you the first time we met."

"Yeah. You took me by surprise, and it overshadowed my usual suave manners." She hoped her expression showed she was teasing, but she couldn't be sure since Callie didn't give any reaction. "Sorry."

"Don't be. I should have made more of an effort to find someone to let them know why I was there." Callie speared an olive and tossed it into her mouth. "When I'm focused, I tend to move full steam ahead, and sometimes that means not thinking about anything other than my art and making sure it will be perfect when I'm done."

Jordan made short work of what was on her plate and washed it down with half her drink. Today she'd survived on coffee alone. Not one to be shy about the food she ate, Jordan put more on her plate. Callie was busy with her meal, and Jordan took the opportunity to watch her. Her wavy hair was caught up in a loose ponytail at the back of her neck, a few stray strands falling around her face. She didn't need to see her eyes to recall their vivid green. Like grass wet with morning dew. Jordan longed for morning walks with Callie at her side strolling on the beach while holding hands. Of sunsets on the porch followed by passion-filled nights. When she thought of Callie, she wanted all the things she'd never dreamed of having. Now it seemed, that's all she could think of.

"On to another chapter." Jordan finished the last bite. Dreams were for people who deserved them, and her past confirmed she'd done nothing to earn hers coming true. "Life is a fantasy wrapped up in webs of lies." She mumbled under her breath and hoped Callie didn't hear her philosophical rant. Where had she heard the words that served as a reminder of things not being as they seemed? Callie's eyes met hers and the questions she saw in them confirmed she heard every word.

"Why do you say that?"

She took a breath. How long would she continue to ignore what was so plain? She didn't deserve dreams or futile attempts at making her wishes come true. "Because I'm not capable of being the kind of person who can turn dreams into reality." Jordan abruptly stood, almost flipping her chair. She turned away from Callie's probing gaze. A warm hand touched her shoulder.

"You're making mine real, so there's got to be another reason."

Initially, she resisted, but Callie wasn't someone she could easily blow off. She turned to find genuine concern creasing her normally smooth forehead. As much as she wanted to share, she just couldn't. "I…" She wasn't sure how to go forward or how to explain what she was feeling. "I have work to do."

Callie's fingers tightened. "The jobsite is closed. You're off duty the rest of the day." When she started to protest, the fingers of Callie's other hand touched her lips, silencing her. "I'm going to take this stuff inside, then we're going for a walk on the beach. If you can tell me what's causing those shadows you think I don't see, all the better." Callie went to the table and Jordan found the courage to follow.

"Let me help." They worked together stowing food in the cooler and when they reached the stairs Jordan carried it inside. Callie changed into calf-length leggings and a long sleeve T-shirt and joined her on the porch, not saying anything. Instead, she grasped her hand, entwined their fingers, and led her down the walk. When was the last time she'd let a woman lead her anywhere? As she thought about it, even the toxic lover she'd had never *led* her. She'd demanded and demeaned until she got her way, which was all the time. Being led by Callie was a much different feeling. They reached the boardwalk and removed their shoes. It took her a bit longer to unlace her short boots, but Callie didn't seem to mind the wait. She stood looking at the waves, her shoulders relaxed, her hands loose at her sides. When she finished taking off her boots, they took the closest path and trudged through the warm sand until they reached the hard-packed surface. Callie produced a canvas bag, and they dropped their shoes in before Jordan slung the straps over her shoulder. Callie's hand reached for hers. This time it was Jordan who entwined their fingers.

"Left or right?" she asked.

"Left." Callie smiled.

The silence was broken by the sound of the waves roaring to the shore and the sea gulls flying overhead, their backdrop the endless blue sky. With tourist season over, there weren't many people about and she was grateful for the relatively deserted beach.

"I'm not sure where to start."

"Where it matters most." Callie gave a little squeeze for reassurance.

Jordan nodded, more to herself than Callie. "My first and last relationship wasn't anything I'm proud of. It was toxic from the start, but I didn't recognize it because it was also new and exciting. Shelley was pretty, fun to be around, and the sex…" This was proving to be harder than she thought. "She used her body to get what she wanted."

"She wanted you."

The sigh that came out was from somewhere deep in her soul. "In the beginning, yes. It didn't change all of a sudden. She was masterful at manipulation. I wanted to make her happy. Then depression set in when she continued to mess with me. I stopped visiting my family because I didn't want anyone to see what poor taste I had by choosing to be with her. Besides, she didn't want them to interfere with 'our time' which was really her time and the things she wanted to do. My life was spiraling into a black hole, and I didn't know how to stop it."

Callie bent down, picked up a small, smooth stone and tucked it in her pocket. "How old were you?"

"Thirty when I started thinking there was something seriously wrong. By then I'd been a mason apprentice for a while. I wanted to follow in my father's footsteps. I would have followed him no matter what he did. He was my idol and my hero." She didn't realize she was crying until her vision blurred and she stumbled.

Callie led them from the water's edge, and they sat on the sun-warmed sand. She was quiet for a few minutes before deciding that if she had any hope of a relationship she needed to be able to talk to Callie about her past. About everything she thought and did. Her nightmare past, but also her dreams and desires, the ones she still didn't feel worthy of.

"Then when my father got sick and was in the hospital…" She swallowed around the knot in her throat, knowing she needed to keep going. "I wanted to be there for him, like he'd always been there for me."

"You weren't?"

She looked at Callie, waiting for her to see the pain in her heart that never left. "Shelley told me he'd be fine. That he didn't need me to feel sorry for him. The one time I visited him, I only stayed a few minutes." Jordan let the memory wash over her, and the pain sliced at her insides like it always did. "Partly because of Shelley and knowing she'd be pissed if I was there too long, and partly because I hated seeing him so frail and…lost." She broke down into sobs and Callie wrapped her arms around her, giving the kind of comfort that was missing from her life. Comfort she should have sought from her mother. She'd been wrong about so much, maybe she'd been wrong about her, too.

"Everyone has regrets, Jordan. Everyone suffers from the what-ifs of their lives. We're human. We make mistakes and there are things we can't see or know until we make them." Callie rubbed her back. "There's not a doubt in my mind that your father knew you loved him."

"I'm not so sure he did. A few months later, he committed suicide."

Callie's breath left her in a gust. "Oh, Jordan. I'm so sorry. But that was his choice. You had nothing to do with it."

Jordan wrestled away and got up. "I had *everything* to do with it. He asked me to stay, and I didn't care enough about him to make the choice. I was stupid and too wrapped up in my own warped relationship to put him first." She whipped around. "Don't you see? What if I'm not capable of making the right decisions, the hard decisions, in any relationship? What if I let someone down like that again?"

Callie stood and came closer, then took her hands. "What if the next time you do make the right decisions? You'll never know how that feels if you don't try."

Callie cupped her cheek and she let herself lean into the touch. It wasn't easy admitting she craved her tender touches more than she'd ever wanted anything for as long as she could remember. Jordan put a little space between them. It wasn't much, but it was enough for her to stop wanting things she couldn't have. "People have been trying to convince me of that for a while without success. But they can't understand the guilt that eats at me. He might still be alive if only I'd been there."

Callie shared a wry smile. "I'm not those people, and I don't give up on causes I believe in." She stepped forward, took her hand, and kept walking toward the far end of the beach. "And you can't know what might have happened if you'd done things differently. None of us can."

As she walked on, Jordan let Callie's words take purchase. The sand began to cool, and she glanced around, needing to find her bearings. She hadn't walked the coastline since she'd been a teenager. After that there'd been other things to hold her interest. Like sports and parties and, at some point, girls. If they kept walking would they reach other states? Could they make it as far as Maine? Would she be able to walk away from the life that haunted her and start again someplace new? Refocusing on the present, Jordan let the warmth of Callie's palm against hers settle into her bones, chasing away the chill of loneliness and the discomfort of the past. It was a rare occasion that she had reason to.

"What about your mother? Do you talk to her or see her?"

Her mother was another touchy subject she shied away from. "Mom and I have never been close." It was hard to remember when they last spoke. "She idolized my oldest brother. He could do no wrong in her eyes." For a minute, the breath froze in her chest. "I never did anything right." She still hadn't called her for her birthday. It was too late now. "I blamed her for not being around the night my father took his life." God, she didn't want the nightmares to start again and hoped talking about it didn't stir up what she'd worked so hard to put to rest, even though her success was minimal.

"Do you think you'll ever be closer to her?"

Jordan shrugged. She'd thought they might find common ground, but the less they talked, the more remote the possibility. That was on both of them. "I won't say it's never going to happen, but I'm not too hopeful." She was just as guilty of keeping her distance as her mom. Maybe she could try to bridge the gap.

"Tell me about the days you don't work. What do you do?"

Callie must have sensed her need to move to a different topic, and she appreciated her ability to read Jordan. She might have good reason to keep some things from Callie, but what she wanted even more was to be honest, because honesty built trust and there were very few people she put her faith in. "There was a time I'd sit in a bar most of the day then stumble home."

"And now?"

"Now I go to the bar, eat, then stumble home." Jordan gave her a tiny grin and Callie laughed. "Kidding. It depends on my mood mostly. Sometimes my best friend, Mel, and I get together and check out a show or take a drive. She's been a lifesaver." Jordan thought about the spirals of deep depression that had surrounded her, knowing if Mel hadn't been there, she likely wouldn't have survived. Then where would she be? Certainly not spending time with Callie.

"I'd like to meet her sometime." Callie walked to the edge of the water and let the waves cover her feet. "Come on. It's great." She smiled, and the glow of her exuberance lit her face.

"It's freezing by now." The Atlantic had a very short warm-water life and even less with the ice caps melting. Jordan had done a lot of late summer dipping in her time, and she still remembered how she'd been chilled to the bone the last time. She was way beyond the antics of her youth. Mostly.

"I didn't think big, strong butches let a little thing like cold water bother them. Guess I was wrong." Callie faced the ocean again.

Jordan grumbled as she rolled up her jeans as far as she could and grabbed Callie from behind, lifting and spinning as she squealed, kicked, and laughed. "Big, strong butches can do lots of things." She spun as water splashed around her ankles and then she zeroed in on Callie's lips before capturing them. The kiss was as exceptional as the first one and she took her time, savoring every nuance of it. The softness of Callie's mouth, the press of her tongue, the wet heat inside. Then the deep, rumbling moan that might have been from her. She set Callie on her feet and came up for air as they panted in harmony.

"Are your feet cold?"

"I don't know. I can't feel anything past my waist." Jordan wanted her and the feeling was apparently mutual because Callie's smile turned molten.

"Let's head back."

Trying to read the expression on Callie's face was difficult. Maybe if she could see her eyes she'd be able to decipher what she was thinking. Jordan decided whatever Callie had in mind, she'd go with it. It was time, as Mel so eloquently put it, she got back into the world of the living.

They skirted the water's edge in comfortable silence, their toes occasionally tickled by salt water. She imagined Callie was lost in thought much like she was. There was plenty to think about, and whether she admitted it or not, the idea of seeing more of Callie... of touching her...was making her a little crazy and a lot wet. It was easy to keep blaming the past on her lackluster present, but how long could she use that excuse as a reason to keep her distance? Especially with someone she wanted to know in every possible way. As she walked up to the front of Callie's house, she took a deep breath that came from her soul. There wasn't any reason to be nervous, except this was Callie and the last thing she wanted was to do something she'd regret. She smiled as Callie unlocked the door while she gave herself a pep talk and heard Mel's voice cheering her on.

❖

Callie was second-guessing her decision as Jordan followed her inside. Denying she didn't want Jordan in all the ways that mattered was pointless. She was a hot, sexy, butch of the kind that always caught her attention, and Jordan made her weak in the knees. And God, the woman could kiss. Like take your breath away, forget your own name kind of kissing. Afraid Jordan would change her mind if she let go, she pulled her along to the kitchen, grabbed bottles of water and headed down the hallway. As they stood outside her bedroom door, consideration of Jordan's feelings kicked in. She didn't want her to think she didn't have a voice, or a choice, about what Callie so desperately wanted. She placed her hand in the middle of Jordan's chest and looked into her questioning eyes.

"I want to make love with you, but only if you want that, too."

Jordan's hand rose and her fingertips drew a line of fire down her cheek. "It's kind of you to ask, but I wouldn't be standing here if I didn't." Jordan smiled before she kissed her. Her lips were soft yet firm. Yielding yet in command.

She broke away breathless, her chest heaving and her body screaming for more of what Jordan offered. She stepped into her room and Jordan followed. Callie closed the door, more out of habit than need. There were no prying eyes to shut out. Her bedroom walls reflected the fire of the setting sun, casting orange and red upon the buttery yellow. She'd had a hard time deciding on the color, but in the end, she went with what she liked. Jordan was someone she liked, too. Jordan's voice, deep and rich, reached her.

"Are you having second thoughts?" Jordan stepped in front of her, understanding and maybe a bit of sadness in her expression.

"No." She took a step closer. "I was thinking how the setting sun made the walls look like fire." She unbuttoned her capris before drawing the zipper down. "And about how much I need your touch."

Jordan visibly shivered and she let out a low moan. "I think I can manage that." Jordan reached for the hem of her shirt and slowly lifted the material upward, then slid her hands beneath it. Her fingertips were rough, but her palms were smooth. "I would have put lotion on if I knew I would be touching you."

Callie wrapped her arms around Jordan's neck. "I don't mind." She rose on tiptoes to press her lips gently to Jordan's and savored the pressure against hers, pulling her closer against her body. She was the one shivering now. There were times when she heeded the warnings of friends and family about not rushing into a relationship, and she'd mostly followed that advice, until now. Jordan was the first person she'd thought of forming anything past a pleasant night with. Still, she didn't want to lose focus of the bigger picture. The one where her business flourished, and she was doing what she enjoyed while earning a living. The idea of sharing that dream beyond the renovation with Jordan was thrilling and scary at the same time, but she was willing to go slow and explore whatever was growing between them. Jordan's mouth moved to her ear, her hot breath flaming the fire burning inside.

"Tell me what you want, Callie." Jordan's tongue stroked below her ear to the sensitive spot that drove her crazy.

She slid her hands over Jordan's shoulders and down her chest, resting just above her breasts. Jordan's heart beat beneath them in strong, fast thuds like a drum, matching her own rhythmic tempo. Jordan nipped at her lips before slipping her shirt all the way off. She cupped her breasts and bit down on her prominent nipples hidden under the fabric of her bra. Her knees buckled under the intensity, and she grabbed Jordan's forearms to keep upright.

Jordan wrapped her arms around her and lifted her onto the bed. "I'd never let you fall, baby," she said, then lowered herself on top, her thighs locking Callie's between them. The kiss was languid at first, a slow sweep of tongues and lips. The passion built with each passing minute. Jordan broke away, desire clearly visible in her hazy, half-closed eyes. "Can we take off our clothes? I want to feel your skin next to mine."

A persistent vision of Jordan often filled her nighttime fantasies and in each one, Jordan's body remained blurry, a mystery she wanted to solve. "Yes."

Callie sat up and removed her bra, then helped Jordan get free of her shirt and the tight tank top beneath. Her breasts were full and high, with dark brown areolas and erect nipples. When Jordan moved to the side of the bed to shed the rest of her clothes, Callie lay back and wriggled out of her pants and panties. Excitement coated her thighs. Granted, it had been months since she'd slept with a woman, but this was more than uncomplicated sex. There were feelings involved. Not that they'd had a lot of in-depth conversations, but Callie was pretty good at reading people and she was fairly certain Jordan felt the same way. The bed dipped and Jordan reclined next to her, and the sight of her body took Callie's breath away.

"I've been wanting to do this since I kissed you. I wasn't sure I'd ever get the chance." Jordan's fingertips danced along her thigh. The touch was light, sensual. Just the kind of touching that drove her insane and wanting for much more. She was in trouble, and she didn't care.

"I'm not going to change my mind, Jordan. Don't make me beg...unless you like that sort of thing."

Jordan growled low in her throat and rolled on top of her, pinning her down with her weight. "I'm not going to make you beg, but I do want to hear you scream." She captured her lips and there was nothing tentative in the kiss that followed. It was possessive and firm with Jordan's hungry mouth opening to press her tongue inside. The slide along hers set her body into orbit, even more than it already was. "Is there anything you don't want me to do?"

Right now there wasn't a single thing she could think of. "Not unless I tell you to stop." Callie wondered if she was the kind of woman Jordan normally slept with. She wanted more than just sex from Jordan, although that was foremost since they were in bed. Would Jordan understand she didn't go for casual even after telling her she wanted to slow down? A one-night stand might have been okay in the past, but she hoped Jordan didn't want that from her. Only time would tell if she was making a mistake.

CHAPTER SEVENTEEN

Callie's mouth was sweet, and her skin tasted like sun-warmed honey. The kind Jordan remembered having as a child. Callie gasped and dug her fingers into her hips and Jordan rose on her forearms to look upon the most beautiful woman she'd ever seen.

"Are you okay?"

"God, you can kiss." Callie's hands slowly ran up and down her sides.

"Is that a bad thing?"

Callie smiled and nipped at her chin. "Only when I can't breathe."

Jordan moved her thigh and pressed against Callie's center, and the warm wet heat that greeted her made her mouth water. "Then I'll give you a break," she said before covering the stiff peak beneath her with her mouth. The tight knot pebbled as she licked and sucked while she played her fingers over Callie's other nipple, slowly working it tighter and tighter.

"You're going to make me come if you keep doing that." Callie fisted her hair and tugged.

The motion wasn't unwelcome because Jordan liked a little rough play now and then. "Isn't that what you want?" She pressed her lips between Callie's breasts and went for another of those soul-deep kisses. Time stood still as the kiss turned from hot to atomic and she wasn't prepared when Callie pushed her shoulder and flipped her onto her back.

"Turnabout is fair play," Callie said. She sat up, straddling her hips, and began massaging her breasts, squeezing with just enough pressure to make her center clench. "I can see how much you like what I'm doing." Callie softly bit each nipple. "I want to know what else you like."

Jordan was about to respond when Callie moved lower, coating her stomach with her essence. She settled between her thighs and looked along her body at her with a heat so intense she knew she'd never felt this much desire directed at her from anyone she'd ever slept with. Callie's long waves trailed over her skin as she moved her head to place kisses on her inner thighs and pushed them wider apart. She wanted Callie's mouth on her, and her body shook in anticipation. "What you're doing is good." She could barely breathe when Callie's tongue swiped the length of her, and her hips rose, chasing the pleasure.

"And now?" Callie's gaze met hers.

"Oh, yeah. That's good, too." She took a breath to steady her racing heart. If she wasn't mindful she would get lost in sensation, and Jordan didn't want to miss one touch from Callie. When Callie moaned, she had all she could do to hold back from letting go. That was what she was used to doing with women who were strangers, or so casual neither batted an eye when it turned out to be a one and done thing. She hoped Callie already knew that wasn't the case between them, and she had to find a way to be sure Callie didn't think otherwise. Right now though, she had her head between her legs doing all sorts of deliciously taunting things to her and that's where she wanted her attention to be.

"What are you thinking?"

Shit. How long had she been drifting? "That there's a gorgeous woman making my body tingle and I don't want to come and end it."

"I don't think you have to worry about that. There's going to be a lot more and I'm in no hurry." Callie flicked over her stone hard clit and Jordan felt it all the way to the hair on her head. "Guess you don't know I love a challenge, and that sounded like one to me." Callie spread her hand below her belly button and applied enough pressure to keep her from moving while she licked and sucked in so many different ways Jordan lost track. It quickly became apparent she didn't stand a chance, and when Callie slid her finger inside her, the full torrent of her orgasm shot through her until a thousand pinpoints of light blazed on the inside of her eyelids.

❖

Callie listened to the rhythmic beating of Jordan's heart. After she'd made her come so hard, Jordan had motioned for her to join her, wrapping her thick arm around her and pulling her close before falling asleep. The idea of how much she enjoyed giving Jordan pleasure that she'd passed out in satiated bliss was the ultimate compliment, and she smiled. Of course, she hoped it was temporary because her center was still slick and throbbing and she longed for Jordan's touch. Only then would her body calm and put an end to her runaway imagination. She hadn't planned on sleeping with her. Well, at least not yet. She wasn't someone who made plans for sex even if she'd thought about it close to a hundred times since meeting Jordan, though she wasn't counting. Jordan had been skittish, and now Callie knew why. Jordan had been afraid she'd fail Callie in some way. Whatever it was, she hoped Jordan was over it. She moved her hand to the center of Jordan's chest, making her stir.

"Hey." Jordan rubbed her back then pulled her closer. "Sorry I crashed."

"Did you enjoy getting there?"

Her fingers cupped her chin until she could catch her gaze. "If it wasn't apparent, you ought to know you rocked me." Jordan pulled her higher and kissed her with careful tenderness.

Kissing Jordan was an experience like no other. The press of her lips, the brush of her tongue, the gentle but insistent probing that somehow became deeper and more demanding, eventually stealing her breath. When she struggled for air, she broke away, her chest heaving and her center longing.

"I want to make love to you." Jordan's thumb traced her swollen lip.

"I want that, too." Her heart pounded in her chest. If her kisses were any indication, Jordan would be a methodical, slow lover and Callie was all for drawn out. Of course, she wasn't above begging if it went on too long. She had nothing against quick, intense sex, but not for the first time with someone because it was a "first impression" kind of thing, and she needed to know a woman was willing to spend time and attention on her. She needed to know those things about Jordan, particularly. It wasn't based on fact, but there was hope their relationship continued to grow after tonight, because if it didn't, Callie wasn't sure she could handle it without showing her disappointment.

Jordan turned her onto her back before reclining on her side next to her, resting on her forearm. She slowly caressed one shoulder, then her collarbone, outlining the peaks and valleys. When she was done, Jordan walked her fingers between her breasts, and her already hard nipples pebbled in anticipation. Ignoring them for the moment, Jordan moved downward and cupped her hip, then moved onto her thigh before sitting up so she could reach her calf. She scooted lower and began to massage her foot.

"A woman's body should be worshipped," Jordan said as she glanced up to meet her gaze, then returned her attention to what she was doing. "Feet are often neglected, but I don't understand why. They carry us through life." Jordan finished the left and moved on to the right. Her touch was firm, and her thumbs pressed spots that Callie hadn't known needed attention.

"That feels wonderful." She did her best to hide her impatience about being touched in other places. Places that longed for whatever gratification Jordan was certain to provide. As if reading her mind, Jordan answered her question.

"I'm going to be touching you a lot, but I wanted you to know I'm not interested in only touching you for sexual pleasure. I want to map your body, learn what you like, see how I can help you relax." Jordan finished her foot and continued upward, mirroring what she'd done on the other side, but this time when she reached her chest, she rose over her and lowered until their bodies were pressed together. "I want you so much the ache is bone deep. Can you feel it, Callie? Can you hear my body calling to yours and asking you to show me what you enjoy?"

For all the times Jordan was stoic, this was the most open and vulnerable she'd ever witnessed. Maybe there wouldn't be anything more between them, but she pushed the thought away, content with the here and now. Her eyes shimmered with emotion and her body trembled against her. "I hear you. Please don't make me wait any longer."

Jordan dipped her head and kissed her like there was no tomorrow. Lost for the umpteenth time, she wasn't ready for Jordan's fingers unerringly finding her slick center, and they moaned in unison at the touch.

"You're so ready for me." Jordan pressed her lips to her neck and traced her pounding pulse. She slipped two fingers inside, filling her the way she longed for.

"Oh God, Jordan. I'm not going to last." She didn't want to explode like some hormone-driven teenager who couldn't wait, but Jordan's kisses were a catalyst to her excitement, and since she'd already waited the long weeks for where she was now, her body had plans of its own.

"Mmm…it's okay. I'll take my time drawing out your pleasure after." Jordan's hot mouth found her nipple and she gently sucked and stroked with her tongue. Callie envisioned her mouth on her wanton center, coaxing her to let go.

She dug her fingers into Jordan's arm and cried out, an explosion of sparks forming on the inside of her eyelids. Her hips continued to chase Jordan's pumping fingers, wanting the feeling to never end. Jordan slipped out and cupped her still trembling flesh gently in her palm. It was an intimate touch and far more meaningful than Callie expected. Unsure what to say, she went with the truth. "Wow." She winced at how lame that single word sounded. It might be okay for fireworks or the price tag on a car, but a mind-altering orgasm deserved better. Jordan kissed her softly then slid onto her side.

"I'm glad you enjoyed it." She kissed her again. "I hope you're not one and done, because that's the last thing I'm thinking."

Somehow she rallied from her state of bliss and rolled to face her. "I might need a little reprieve, but I'm far from done with you." Callie moved her hand over Jordan's bulging bicep, scratching lightly with her short nails before trailing over her tight abdomen and gave a push. Jordan's eyes narrowed as she got the hint to lie flat.

"What do you have in mind for me?" Her tone was playful while her eyes revealed anticipation.

She leaned over, her lips close to Jordan's. "Well," she began, "I thought I'd start here." Callie pressed her lips to Jordan's slightly parted ones and slipped her tongue inside, eliciting a moan. After exploring and tasting until they were both breathless, she pulled away and smiled.

"That was a nice start." Jordan caressed her back, her thighs.

"Then here." She moved her mouth over one puckered nipple, closed her teeth enough to capture it, and tugged.

"Oh, Christ." Jordan's hips lifted.

"Mmm...you like?" Callie repeated on the other side, eliciting another oath. "I think you do." She straddled Jordan so she could massage both at the same time. Jordan held on to her hips and she pulled her down for a scathing kiss. She broke away and smiled. "Nuh-uh. I'm calling the shots now." Callie lifted and skimmed her hand between them. Jordan was wet and hard beneath her fingers.

"Callie, please."

The more she stroked along her hot center the more Jordan's eyes lost focus, but she didn't want her to come. Not like this. She shimmied lower until she settled between Jordan's firm thighs. Jordan's enticing scent filled her as she inhaled. She was swollen and glistening as Callie tasted her, making Jordan's groan renewed.

"Oh, yeah, make me come, baby." Jordan's fingers found hers, her hips thrusting forward with each swipe of her tongue.

Jordan's excitement and obvious pleasure spurred her on to give her what they both wanted…an explosive orgasm. She sucked the length of Jordan's stiff clit between her lips and flicked her tongue over the tip.

"Shit."

Jordan's fingers threaded through her hair, lightly grabbing and guiding. She wasn't rough, but Callie could tell how close she was. Excited by Jordan's reaction to her ministrations, moisture pooled between her thighs. It wasn't long before Jordan's stomach tightened as she moaned a deep, guttural sound followed by utter stillness before her entire body shook with her climax. Callie continued to coax more from her until Jordan gently pushed her away.

"No more, babe." Jordan guided her into her arms again and held her close. "You're amazing."

Callie rested her hand between Jordan's breast. "I could say the same thing about you."

"Yeah, but I said it first," Jordan said in a teasing tone.

She play-poked her, making Jordan flinch, then laugh. "For someone who doesn't have a lot of comebacks, you've suddenly found your voice."

Jordan's gaze softened. "What can I say, you bring out the best in me."

Jordan smoothed her hand over her hip, stirring her center to life with the intimate gesture. She could get used to more evenings like this, but that might not be anything Jordan was interested in. Callie had the feeling Jordan kept women at a distance, and that could end up being a problem for both of them because Callie had no interest in being a one-night stand.

CHAPTER EIGHTEEN

Jordan expected there would be an awkward silence once the sex was over between her and Callie, but nothing could have been further from reality. As she cuddled Callie to her, luxuriating in the softness that followed an incredible orgasm, she had the sense of a calm she hadn't ever enjoyed after being in bed with a woman. She'd been even more surprised by the easy banter and how the quiet stretches were the result of one or both dozing off in the afterglow. At least, she hoped it was from being physically satisfied, otherwise she was going to have to up her game if they did this again.

Her eyes popped open. Would they sleep together again? What was Callie looking for? Or maybe she wasn't looking for anything. Maybe all she'd done was reach out to her in a moment of compassion and that was all there would ever be between them. Maybe it had been some kind of pity sex after Jordan had shared her history with her. The thoughts kept coming, battering her, growing with every minute until she couldn't breathe.

"Shit." Jordan threw back the sheet as she rolled out of bed. In the early morning hours, she mumbled an apology, saying she needed to go home at some point so she could get ready for work. Callie hadn't seem bothered by the news. In fact, she'd kissed Jordan soundly before drifting off again, leaving her to make her escape without the endless stream of excuses for her departure she usually made. That alone was a relief.

Once she was home, Jordan fixed the coffee and headed for the shower, contemplating the day ahead. With the water adjusted, she stepped under the stream and let the heat envelop her. After doing jobsite rounds she had to see Callie, and she wasn't sure how she felt about the whole thing. What if what they'd done last night was simply the usual physical release and nothing more? The kind of thing she wouldn't think twice about normally. That wasn't true with Callie. She not only knew her, but she was also fascinated by her intelligence and her kind nature, not to mention her innate beauty. She'd known what Jordan needed even when Jordan hadn't, and there'd not been anyone other than Mel who touched her soul as deeply and in a totally new way.

When she slid her soapy sponge over her breasts, her mind filled with visions of a naked Callie and all of the exploration she'd done on Jordan's body. Of course, she'd done her own exploring, reveling in the lush curves and softness, so different from her own harder, rougher body. Her clit surged at the memory. She opened her eyes and hurriedly finished. She couldn't let herself get caught up in one night. Jordan didn't want to fixate on what came next, but at some point they needed to talk about it. Experience taught her to face the hard stuff because not facing it made it harder. She didn't want to admit she'd be disappointed if Callie stepped back. For now it was better to keep her focus on the one incredible night they'd shared and leave it at that.

Jordan stood in her closet shaking her head. *I really need to do laundry.* She briskly slid hangers back and forth before settling on a pair of faded, distressed jeans and a long-sleeved T-shirt with her company name emblazoned on the back. The upper left side of the front, in smaller script had her name. By running her fingers through her hair, she'd done nothing but redistribute the unruly curls into something less sloppy...but only a little. Methodically fixing a travel mug by adding a little sugar, then cream before pouring in the coffee reminded her of the methodical way she'd mapped and memorized Callie's body last night, how she hoped she'd have another opportunity to learn more because she desperately wanted more. Thinking about how her feelings might not be shared by Callie was a sobering thought that didn't help improve her mood.

Being in her truck gave her a sense of purpose and the routine of reviewing her clipboard settled her overactive mind from the constant questioning of how wise it had been to sleep with Callie. Not that she regretted it. Far from it. But they'd become friends and the possibility that she'd messed that up, like she had so many things in her life, left her anxious. But then she remembered Callie had initiated the intimacy, so could she really blame herself for accepting the offer?

Time whizzed by as she maneuvered through the heavy traffic and before she knew it, she was pulling into the parking lot of a semi-finished strip mall. She'd been lucky to score the high-priced, low-risk commercial project. Not only was it fairly close to home, but there was also the bonus of it being flanked on both ends by food businesses, making the mechanical portion fairly easy to plan. One, a café and bakery, the other a soon-to-be quaint American restaurant serving lunch and dinner. *Dinner.* Would Callie be up for dinner out, like on a real date? Should she ask? God, she was getting way ahead of herself. One night of outrageously satisfying sex didn't mean they were dating. Or exclusive. But then, it didn't mean they weren't dating, either. Her chest tightened as her vision blurred and Callie's naked body beneath some faceless stranger made her cringe. She pushed the vision and thoughts of dating out of her mind. It was time to focus on what she was paid to do.

Clipboard in hand, Jordan strode toward the bakery, knowing it should be in the final stages of completion and she was ready to kick some ass if it wasn't. It was quiet as she entered the front door, ominously so. The upper half of the walls had been painted a pale yellowish-green, some odd shade of chartreuse that she would never have chosen for a bakery, but the proprietors got to decide on the décor and she was fine with that. Jordan took her time inspecting and making sure there was nothing that needed to be corrected as she perused her notes.

In the back, behind the counter and out of direct sight of the customers, the kitchen was a bit sparse, but gleamed white. Appliances hadn't been installed yet, and she made a note to check if they'd been ordered or if there'd been a shipment delay. While some of the country had begun to recover from the pandemic, construction materials still lagged behind. Some tradesmen didn't make it out of the hospital, and manufacturing had come to a near screeching halt as materials and labor had suffered…still suffered…from a shortage of workers. Moms and dads who had decided to do something else as they looked after their children who'd been forced to attend school remotely were a big part of that workforce. This wasn't the only time she'd thought about how her father would have managed in the first year when everything came to a near halt and materials were backlogged. What would he have done to keep his family from starving and a roof over their heads? That had always been his biggest concern when she was growing up and hadn't changed when she got older. It wasn't like he had other skills he could rely on. Being ex-navy and without a high school diploma, his prospects would have been bleak, especially since so many businesses closed, if only to wait out the storm. She briefly offered a second of thanks he hadn't had to deal with any of that, but the recurring hurt and anger assaulted her anew and she had to take a minute to breathe through it. Maybe talking to Callie about the past hadn't been such a good idea after all.

"Jordan, are you okay?" George, plumber extraordinaire, stood in the doorway of a small but functional restroom. This one had "Customers" stenciled in an ornate script on the freshly painted door. There was a twin restroom marked "Employees only" next to it.

She finally snapped out of her mental road trip. "Hey, George. How's it going?" she asked, while ignoring his inquiry. What would she say? He stared at her for a couple of beats before responding.

"Just finishing the sink hook-ups, then my job is done." George shared a smile, causing the lines in his face to deepen.

"Great. This one looks about finished then." She pretended to be reading her clipboard, still lost in memories of her father and how much she continued to miss him every day. Guilt and longing warred inside.

"I'm heading over to the restaurant next. You want to follow me?"

Concern was evident in George's eyes, and she knew she'd failed to appear like she'd gotten her shit together. Nothing new there.

"You go ahead. I'll meet up with you in a few. I haven't been to the other three businesses between here and there in a couple of days."

George nodded and headed out. Finally alone, Jordan had to admit she wasn't mentally prepared for a relationship though convincing the rest of her would probably be more difficult. She did a quick walkthrough before she moved to the next retail space. All the while she wondered how much she'd fucked up whatever was between her and Callie.

❖

Callie pulled the sheets from the bed a few hours after Jordan's too early departure. She supposed she should have asked her to stay, or at least gotten up and walked her to the door, but she was enjoying the languid afterglow and was too tired to do more than plant a grateful kiss on her swollen lips. She lifted the sheets and inhaled Jordan's lingering scent as it clung to the fibers and mixed with the smell of sex. She couldn't help smiling as visions of their lovemaking flashed through her meandering mind.

Jordan was a self-assured lover, her actions were without the hesitancy she glimpsed in other settings. The revelation of her guilt and the death of her father made sense for some of her resistance and, certainly, her reluctance to share that kind of knowledge was understandable. Callie's heart had ached at the defeated, devastated look on Jordan's face. Then, when she broke down into sobs of despair, all Callie could think of was easing her self-inflicted punishment for a crime she hadn't committed.

With the laundry started and a plan for the morning, she fixed herself a bagel and took it and her coffee out to the sun-warmed porch. She laughed when her stomach rumbled, having worked up an appetite through the night. She also wasn't in any hurry to wash away Jordan's scent from her body and the soreness of her muscles was a pleasant reminder it had been a while since she'd been physically engaged with a woman for an entire night.

The breeze was pleasantly cool and missing the humidity that had hung on for days during the previous month. She wasn't sorry to see them go. Inhaling the salty air, Callie was once more thankful she'd made the decision to move there. Sure, she didn't know what winter or early spring would be like. There was always the danger of an oceanic storm and the surge that accompanied it, but she'd done her research and they had been rare, though with the climate change every location was dealing with, she also knew those statistics might change dramatically in the years to come. If it became too often, she could move inland and away from the coast altogether. The idea of not seeing Jordan often, if at all, made her stomach clench unpleasantly and she pushed the thought away. She stood abruptly as if moving would keep it at a distance.

Folding laundry had always been a mindless task, both orderly and necessary, and Callie looked down to find only one shirt left in the basket. With the sheets in the dryer and the rest of the house picked up, she finally headed to the shower. When the warm water sluiced over her shoulders and back, Callie imagined Jordan's warm hands in its wake, her fingertips pressing and searching for the places that made her sigh or moan or excited her more than her hard, hot body did. The water began to run cool, and she wondered how long she'd been lost in the daydream.

After applying lotion and drying her hair, Callie pulled on a pair of worn, skintight work-out pants and a near threadbare T-shirt. Even though the morning started cool, the forecast called for a high in the mid-seventies, and the inside of the garage still lacked air conditioning, though the additional windows helped with ventilation. She glanced at the clock. Since it was almost noon Jordan would likely arrive soon, but she wasn't sure how she'd be feeling following their night of passion. She refused to analyze it, instead focusing on how wonderful it had felt being in Jordan's arms. Her phone sat on the counter, abandoned since last evening. Without giving herself a chance to change her mind, she pressed the speed number. The thought of Jordan purposefully avoiding her call banged around in her head and made her stomach flutter in an unpleasant way, but after four rings the gravelly voice on the other end soothed her nerves.

"Morning," Jordan said.

Now that she had her on the line she wasn't quite sure what to say. "Hey," she said, then rolled her eyes. If that was the best she could come up with she was going to have to work on her morning after skills. "It's lunchtime and I was wondering if you would be heading over soon."

"Oh, that late already?"

Callie imagined Jordan running her hand over her face, the way she often did when perplexed, and she smiled. "Afraid so."

"Give me thirty minutes or so. Some assho..." Jordan paused. "I've got an issue that needs clearing up, so I might be a little longer, but I'll be there."

Relief flooded in at the absence of regret in Jordan's voice. "I'll throw something together for us to eat."

"Okay. See you in a bit."

Jordan's words might not have relayed warm fuzzies, but that was okay. She didn't think that was Jordan's style and she wondered what her ultimate style was.

CHAPTER NINETEEN

The day turned warmer than Jordan had expected and sweat dripped down her back. Not for the first time she thought about taking off her outer shirt, but she was having a case of shyness with Callie that wasn't like her at all. When she'd arrived at the house Callie had met her with a tight hug and a lingering kiss, sending all the doubts she'd been harboring skittering back to the shadows of her mind. Then after a quick bite to eat, they'd gone straight to work, with plenty of small touches and teasing throughout the afternoon.

"Are you sure I can't get you something else to wear? You look like you're about to pass out."

That wasn't far from the truth. She felt the heat in her face, the slick coat of sweat gluing her clothes to her skin. "Fuck it," she grumbled under her breath, pulling and yanking until she stood in her sports bra and caught the tiniest bit of breeze that helped cool her down. She let out an audible sigh of relief and Callie giggled.

"You should have done that hours ago."

Their gazes locked. Callie licked her lips after scanning Jordan's torso and that look was the one she'd both been hoping for and dreading. She wasn't beyond enjoying an appreciative glance in her direction, but coming from Callie made it even more so since she already knew about the parts still hidden. Her clit tightened and she turned away, needing to get herself back on track following the intensity of Callie's open ogling.

"Jordan?"

Inhaling first, she turned to face a smiling Callie and couldn't help smiling in return.

"Catch."

Callie tossed a bottle of water and she snatched it out of the air. It was ice-cold, and she cracked the seal before taking a couple of refreshing gulps. "Thanks."

"You're welcome." Callie sat on the bench she'd found at a garage sale and stared at the newly painted walls. "This color palette is so much nicer. I never would have painted the walls beige if the five-gallon bucket hadn't been ridiculously cheap." Callie faced her. "Thanks for suggesting that the showroom should reflect the artist. You were right."

Praise wasn't something Jordan enjoyed very often, mainly because the haunted feelings wouldn't allow her to, but she gave herself permission to bask in Callie's words, even if only for a few precious minutes. "You would have gotten there if you weren't being frugal. My guess is you were going for fresh and clean at the time." She stepped down off the ladder and turned to face Callie. "This," she said, waving at the space, "is your baby. I'm just glad I was here to help see it through and shape it into your dream place." Jordan took in the transformation and a sense of pride swelled inside before her anxiety rose. With it being early October and the holidays approaching, Callie might be open in time to catch the off-season vacationers who would sporadically come and go until Thanksgiving, when the tourists dwindled even more. The former garage was almost done, and she couldn't help thinking about the implications. They hadn't talked about last night though she'd caught glimpses of Callie studying her, and foolish as it might be, she'd let herself hope their time together would continue past the project. It was likely wishful thinking on her part and the familiar sadness enveloped her before Callie's hand found hers and she tugged her around. She gazed into Callie's eyes and her breath caught.

"Are you sorry about last night?"

"What? No!" She brushed her fingertips over Callie's cheek, loving how soft and warm her skin was.

"Then why have you been dancing around talking about it? About us?"

"Because it's been so long since I've wanted more than one night with a woman, I didn't want to know if that's all it was." She regretted saying out loud what she'd been thinking all along, and yet, there was some relief letting it out, too.

"Is that what you think I want? One night and then we go our separate ways?" Callie studied her intensely.

"Honestly, I don't know." Her insides trembled while externally she stood planted to the spot, prepared for the blow of disappointment that would certainly come, like it always had.

Callie tipped her head. "I think," she said as she raised up on tip toes and planted a gentle kiss on her mouth. "That neither of us are feeling as we usually do."

She was going to give some line of denial. One that would usually keep a woman at arm's length...or farther. But Callie wasn't just any woman and Jordan didn't feel distant like she normally did after she'd slept with someone. While her track record sucked, she wasn't about to pull Callie down the road of broken dreams with her. She'd pictured herself working side by side with her father and setting up their own construction crew with the money she managed to tuck away here and there ever since she began working in high school. She never got the chance to share that dream with her father. She'd waited too long. And what about the dream she'd all but given up on, about finding that special someone to share her life with? What if she hesitated to share the things that mattered to her with Callie before it was too late? "I can't make you promises I might not be able to keep."

"I'm not asking for any." Callie's hand moved to the center of her chest. "Let's not get ahead of ourselves. I like your company. Last night was fantastic." After she nodded in agreement Callie went on. "Can't we just enjoy where we are without forcing anything we might not be ready for?"

Jordan's hammering heart revealed that she was both relieved and disappointed. She had hoped Callie would push for answers because she didn't want to be in limbo, but Callie was right. It was way too soon for either of them to think last night sealed the deal on a relationship she wasn't sure she could live up to, and apparently Callie agreed. Without examining what she was doing, Jordan wrapped her arm around Callie's waist and pulled her closer. "Does that mean we can have dinner soon, and maybe a repeat of last night sometime?"

A smile lit up Callie's face. "I think that would be wonderful."

There were a lot of characteristics that made Callie special and each one was a reason for her to abandon her hesitancy. Callie deserved a partner who would be supportive and stick around through the rough times, because there were bound to be rough times. Every relationship experienced them. She'd never been good in those instances, but maybe it was time she not give up so soon. After all, if Callie was willing to stick around that meant something. Right?

Jordan began to gather her tools and put the ones she'd no longer need in her truck. The heating and cooling system was due to be installed this week. Callie had suggested putting in a couple of windows in the wall separating the workshop from the showroom. They would go in tomorrow and the modification which would have been easier if they'd thought about it in the beginning, was something she'd done frequently on other jobs. Plus she didn't mind having a reason to be around a bit longer. After that, all she'd have to do were touch ups, if there were any, then she'd be back to her routine of jobsite inspections and putting in bids for future work projects. She wanted a full calendar to take her through until spring. Inside jobs were less plentiful than construction, but she didn't mind traveling to earn a paycheck.

Her father's masonry skills had set her up with a recognizable name, even if people's memories were short and they weren't quite sure where they'd heard it before. The familiar, somewhat diminished anguish of loss stabbed at her chest, and for a minute she forgot to breathe. She should be past this point by now, shouldn't she? Though inside she didn't think she ever would. The pain helped keep his memory alive, even if they weren't the kind of memories she wanted to have. Holding on to the hard ones seemed like a just punishment for not being there...not seeing how much he was suffering. Callie's hand touched hers and the fog of regret dissipated.

"What's wrong?" Callie's fingertips wiped her cheek and came away wet.

She shook her head. She only let herself cry when she was alone, except for when she was with Mel, who'd seen her in a nuclear meltdown more times than she cared to admit, until Callie. And here she was doing it again. What was it about her that made Jordan let go so easily? Safe. Still, what would she think if Jordan couldn't control her stormy emotions? They often snuck up on her at the most inopportune times.

"Memories of sadder times." She shrugged. "Sorry."

"You don't need to apologize. I don't like seeing you so upset is all." Callie's eyes shimmered as though she too was on the brink of tears and Jordan forced a smile she didn't feel.

"Big, bad butch who's prone to bouts of crying probably isn't your idea of someone you want to get involved with." She made a joke of the situation though nothing felt funny.

"I don't have preconceived notions of how a woman should act, except I tend to steer clear of outright assholes." Callie tugged her hand, smiling.

She chuckled. "I'll try to remember to not be an asshole then." They puttered around the space and with a reluctant good-bye Jordan said she'd see her the next day. She wanted to install the windows and make sure they worked correctly. She had to put in the ceiling hooks, unbox and move the furniture Callie was having delivered, and do any last-minute touch ups. Callie hadn't asked for help moving her art supplies and sellable items into the shop, but she'd offer. Some of the items were heavy. Callie was capable of physical labor, she'd proven that during the renovations, but four hands would make the work go quicker. It would also provide her with an opportunity to ask Callie out to dinner to celebrate. It had been ages since she had a reason to celebrate anything, but Callie made her want to do a lot of things she hadn't bothered with in a long time.

CHAPTER TWENTY

Y ou've had sex!" Mel said in her usual analytical fashion. "Jesus, you're crass." Jordan disliked the word being used to describe the relationship between her and Callie as casual or meaningless. For her, it had been a lot more than just sex. She'd let Callie past the rough exterior she used as a barrier to keep people away, and for reasons she'd yet to justify, she hadn't wanted the disconnect when it came to Callie. When she refocused, Mel was staring at her.

"What's different about this mystery woman?"

In no mood to dissect her feelings, she let her annoyance at the inquiry surface. "Can we just drop it?" No way was Mel about to let her get away with the brushoff and she knew it.

Mel lifted her coffee cup and smiled smugly. "Not in this century." Mel emptied her cup and retrieved the carafe, refilling both their mugs before retaking her seat across from her.

"I've been helping Callie renovate her garage to turn it into an art studio and showroom, as you know." Jordan thought back to their initial meeting when she'd been so annoyed. "She..."

"She must be beautiful if you're at a loss for words." Mel leaned forward. "It's such a rare occasion these days."

Jordan's face heated. "Yes, she's beautiful. Funny and open, and—"

"And you can't stop thinking about all the things that might go wrong instead of the things that could go right." Mel stood.

"I'm making breakfast and you're going to wait until it's done and you're going to eat before you run off with your tail between your legs."

She ran her hand over her face. Without a plausible reason to leave, Jordan was stuck listening to Mel's accounting for her actions, all of which made perfect sense. "You know, I expected a little more in the way of privacy."

Mel stopped whipping pancake batter and looked up. "And you thought that why?"

Jordan chuckled. "Wishful thinking?"

"Mm-hmm, not going to happen." While the electric griddle heated up she pulled a bowl from the refrigerator and dumped potatoes with onions into a pan. "Now that you're finishing up, what excuse will you have to spend time with her?"

Jordan's stomach rumbled from the aromas filling the kitchen, but it was quickly followed by an uneasiness that had been foremost since she'd packed up her tools the other day. "I'm not done yet." Of course, the two-day delay in the arrival of the windows had only intensified the impending last day of work at the shop and Mel's words rang true. She'd hoped Callie would jump at the chance to spend more time with her, which was crazy since they'd only known each other for a couple of months. "Callie wants to take it slow."

Mel expertly stirred the potatoes with a flair Jordan never mastered, then sprinkled mini chocolate chips over the batter she'd ladled onto the griddle. "That would be the wisest thing to do," she said as she stood at the ready to flip the bubbly medallions.

Sure, it made perfect sense, yet it was also the last thing Jordan *wanted* to do. "I know, but…" *Fuck it.* "This might be the first time in my life I want to dive headfirst into the unknown and take my chances that everything will work out."

"Dude. Seriously?" Mel put a heaping plate in front of her and set the bottle of maple syrup between them.

She looked directly at Mel. "I know."

Mel wrapped her arm around her shoulder and hugged her hard. "Then go for it."

She closed her eyes and envisioned being next to Callie, touching her, tasting her. Her body surged at the visceral images, but that was something she could control. It was the other part of her that had a mind of its own, and her head had nothing to do with it.

❖

Callie stood in the retail section, her hands on her hips. Jordan was nailing the trim around the newly installed windows. The three-over-three panes lent a nice contrast to the other details that were a bit more modern feeling, and the overall vibe of an eclectic décor satisfied the artist in her. Soon she'd have her grand opening. Jordan had put her in touch with an associate who produced flyers and business cards among other publicity-type materials. They were coming to the shop the day after tomorrow to take pictures and get the lay of the land. She wasn't thrilled about shelling out more money, however having a business that very few people knew about would be worse in the long run. Jordan set down the nail gun and stood next to her.

"What do you think?"

"I think it's perfect." She beamed at the nearly finished space.

Jordan turned to face her. "Perfect." Her eyes sparkled in the fading light and reminded Callie of grains of sand that reflected sunlight the same way. Jordan was only a foot away.

If they both leaned in their lips would meet. She wanted Jordan to kiss her and remind her how glorious her mouth felt pressed to hers, not that she'd forget any time soon. Should she make the first move, or would that give Jordan the impression that she was desperate after telling her to go slow, but what did slow mean for her? For Jordan? She stood on her toes and brushed her lips over Jordan's without lingering and took a step back. The light faded from Jordan's eyes. "I should move supplies in so I can get everything staged for Declan."

It hadn't taken her long to decide to go with them for her promotional needs. They were smart, public-savvy, and professional. Best of all, Declan promised a 48- to 72-hour turnaround time, meaning she'd only be open a day or two before advertising flooded the area. She could live with that.

Jordan stowed miscellaneous items in the truck, then stood next to her. "I can help."

"Haven't you done enough already?" Callie asked. She didn't want to take advantage of Jordan's kindness, especially not when it was pretty obvious people in her past had.

"I don't mind." Jordan shrugged, looking at the ground and seeming lost. Finally, she met her gaze and moved closer. "I thought maybe we should celebrate your studio being done by taking you to dinner."

Butterflies danced happily in her stomach. "That's sweet of you. I was thinking of asking you to dinner to thank you for all your hard work and for putting up with my last-minute changes." She *had* thought about celebrating, along with hoping Jordan wouldn't mind spending the night. A wonderful ending to a beautiful time of her dream business coming to fruition.

Jordan's hand found hers. "Let me this time." Her eyes searched Callie's for a long beat, as though she were asking far more than for a simple dinner date.

Callie tried to read what Jordan wasn't saying. The shadows were missing, so she took it as a good sign. "I'd love to have dinner with you." She squeezed Jordan's hand when what she really wanted to do was slowly kiss her until they were both breathless. Standing so close to Jordan made her rethink all the reasons it made no sense to not follow what her mind and her heart were telling her. Time was short. Life sped by at breakneck speeds. And Jordan…well, Jordan was a skittish colt at times.

"Good. Great." Jordan's smile lit up her face. "Let's get your stuff moved, then I'll leave you to it."

They spent the next hour hauling materials to the workshop. She had a few hours of organizing ahead of her, but instead of dreading it, she was looking forward to the work. Jordan stood off to the side, inspecting one particular wall, a frown creasing her forehead.

"Everything okay?"

"I should have sanded this again before painting."

Jordan ran her hand over the spot and Callie's heart sped up. Jordan's hand moved with purpose, just like it had over her body. Her clit began to tingle, and she wanted Jordan's hand to be on her instead of the wall.

"How does seven o'clock sound?" Jordan's deep tone brought her out of her imaginings.

"That works." Maybe if Jordan wasn't standing there looking all hot and handsome, she could get her shit together and not appear like some star-struck fangirl. Which she definitely was not. Well, not totally, but it wouldn't take much to get her there if she kept fantasizing about all the ways she'd like to experience Jordan's talents.

"I'll see you then." Jordan sprinted for her truck. "Wear comfortable shoes," she said over her shoulder before jumping into the cab. She waved as she backed out, a mischievous grin on her face, leaving Callie to wonder what she'd gotten herself into.

CHAPTER TWENTY-ONE

Jordan hadn't been nervous when she'd invited Callie to dinner. In fact, she'd been more than a little excited to spend time with her, and the idea of being alone together overtook her thoughts until all she could picture was the two of them naked and doing those wonderful things they'd done the first time. As she pulled into Callie's driveway just before seven, Jordan wiped her sweaty palms on her jeans, took a deep breath, and got out. When she looked up, Callie came bounding out of the house and her smile lit up her entire face.

"Hi," Callie said. She was standing so close Jordan could smell her perfume. Something light and clean, like the faint sound of the ocean in the distance. "So, where are we going?"

Jordan glanced down and smiled at the summer white Keds Callie wore. The dress that fluttered around her knees wasn't half bad either. The idea that there was little if anything beneath it made her fingers twitch, and she fought the urge to slide her hand up Callie's thigh to find out. "A little restaurant tucked away in a niche off the beaten path. I thought we could walk and not worry about sharing a bottle of wine if you'd like."

Callie slid her hand into hers and gave a squeeze. "I think that's a marvelous idea." She went on tiptoes and planted a light kiss on her cheek. "Left or right?" They stood at the end of the driveway as Callie looked in both directions.

There weren't too many times that she was tongue-tied, but Callie made her forget everything except being with her and this was no exception. Finally, she found her voice. "Right." The restaurant was a ten-minute walk, just far enough for some easy conversation. "Did you get your shop settled?"

"Mmm…pretty much. I'll have to wait until I'm actually working on something to see if everything is where it should be, but I think it's close."

The idea that Callie might have to lift the heavy totes of glass didn't sit well with her. "If you need help rearranging, please let me know."

Callie stopped and pulled her around. "Jordan, I've been lugging those totes around for a while."

She hadn't meant to make it sound like Callie wasn't capable. From everything she'd seen, she was pretty self-sufficient in that department. "Sorry."

"Hey, don't be sorry. I appreciate you looking out for me, but I'm okay doing some stuff on my own, and when it comes to the shop…well, that's definitely all on me."

Jordan was much the same way when it came to setting up a jobsite. She had a vision and God help the crew member who tried to change things up. There'd been hell to pay more than once, and she hoped by now everyone knew the deal since she hired the same crews for most of her projects. "I get that."

Callie's mouth lifted on one side. "I figured you would."

They continued down Rehoboth Avenue, then turned onto Second Street, stopping here and there to admire the window displays. Callie took out her cell phone and snapped a picture of one.

"This would be a good place to put some pieces of my work."

The gift shop was upscale from the fare on the Boardwalk and displayed more of the quality items that Callie's art deserved to be among. Her chest puffed out a bit. She was happy she'd contributed to Callie's growing commissioned businesses.

"There's a lot more like this one on the way out to route 1A. I could show you sometime if you're interested." She couldn't help wanting to do everything she could to see Callie establish a wide base of retail shops for her wares. Jordan knew how important the success of Callie's art was to her, and exposure to as many buyers as possible would be key to reaching that goal. She turned the corner and pointed. "That's the place. I hope you like Italian." She hadn't thought there might be a cuisine Callie didn't like. "There's a steak house a few blocks farther if you don't."

"Italian and a nice bottle of chianti sounds pretty damn good to me."

It wasn't easy to admit the words Callie spoke along with the gleam in her eyes gave her a thrill like no other. The last few years had marched on without anyone...or anything...to look forward to and now here she was with a beautiful woman who seemed to want to spend time with her. Not just for a drink or two and a quick lay. They were having meaningful, deep conversations buoyed by teasing, laughter, and fun. She could get used to this kind of a relationship, and that was the problem, because as much as she would support Callie's endeavors, she wasn't so sure she could provide the emotional investment a relationship required.

❖

Callie watched as Jordan carried on an animated conversation with the waitress. She could tell it was all in fun and not flirty, not that Jordan couldn't flirt with whomever she wanted even when the idea made her feel a bit like a Doberman protecting her owner, which was ridiculous. She had no claim on Jordan's affection. She was the one who had said they should enjoy the moment. The more she was around Jordan, the more time she wanted to spend with her, which went against everything she'd been content with up till now.

"So," Jordan said. "What looks good to you?"

Heat rose from her chest, and she hoped Jordan didn't notice the flush she felt reach her cheeks. She'd been so busy watching Jordan she hadn't even looked at the open menu in front of her. "Everything sounds wonderful." She met her gaze. "What are you having?"

Jordan smiled, showing off her bright white teeth. "I'm a sucker for their chicken parm, but I might venture into the unknown for a change."

Callie couldn't help but wonder if there was a hidden meaning in Jordan's words. Initially, she'd had the impression that Jordan didn't do relationships, that she only went for casual and uncommitted engagements for the pure pleasure of being with a woman, much like Callie had. Maybe she'd been wrong. She'd certainly been wrong about Jordan's gruff front being her natural tendency, because that wasn't who she really was at all. Callie had been witness to her kindness on more than one occasion, so she knew better. When she refocused, Jordan was still studying her, and the waitress had reappeared tableside. She cleared her throat and pointed to the first thing that caught her eye.

"I'll do the shrimp pomodoro."

"Very good."

"I'll have the orecchiette with broccoli rabe and sausage." Jordan glanced at her. "We'll start with the calamari and a bottle of Banfi Chianti."

The waitress scribbled on her pad. "I'll put this in and bring the wine right over."

Jordan cleared her throat. "I hope you don't mind my ordering. I thought we should have something to eat now if we're going to be drinking."

"You won't hear me complaining." She smiled, and while it wasn't quite forced, it didn't feel genuine either. For a brief moment, Callie wondered if drinking was a good idea. She wasn't sure why wine sometimes went right to her head, and she hoped that wouldn't be the case tonight, not after she'd proven she could get buzzed from wine. She definitely wanted Jordan to come to her house after dinner. Definitely hoped there'd be a repeat of amazing sex. Then she chastised herself for assuming Jordan wanted the same thing.

Tipping her head, Jordan studied her, a look of concentration clearly displayed. "Is something wrong?"

That made her sit up. "No. Why?"

Jordan shrugged. "I don't know. You looked disappointed, maybe."

The waitress brought over the bottle of wine and two glasses, pulled the cork, and poured a tasting into Jordan's glass. She swirled the contents, inhaled, then sipped. After she swallowed she nodded, and the waitress poured in each goblet. "Your appetizer will be out in a few minutes. I'll bring you warm bread with your entrée."

"Thank you." Jordan lifted her glass aloft and waited until she raised hers. "To the start of an evening of stimulating conversation and good food."

Is that all you want from tonight, Jordan? She couldn't help wanting Jordan to be on the same wavelength, where the night ahead held the promise of steamy kisses and sweaty bodies. A shiver traveled up her spine at the visual. "To tonight." Callie wanted to tell Jordan what she was thinking and feeling, but the thought of being presumptuous and how much of a turn off it might be, kept her from verbalizing her desires out loud. That, along with the memory of how sharing her wants and needs with her family had gone, made her refrain from telling Jordan. Later, maybe.

The plate of calamari was placed between them along with small dishes, and the aroma made her mouth water.

Jordan picked up a plate. "May I serve you?"

"Yes, please." She waited until Jordan served herself, then dug in. The coating wasn't heavy, like it sometimes was. The rings were tender, not chewy, with a light crunch and the seasoning brought her tastebuds alive. "Oh my God, this is good."

"I'm glad you like it. Like the chicken parm, I tend to order this every time I eat here." Jordan met her gaze. "When I find something I like I tend to stick with it."

Something in the way she said the words made Callie believe she definitely wasn't talking about food. She swallowed the last piece from her plate and drank some wine. "I'll have to remember that."

"If not, I'll remind you." Jordan smiled.

She helped herself to more and glanced around as she ate, taking in the subdued ocean decorations scattered throughout. The pale blue-and-black checked tablecloths hinted at the cuisine, as did the pictures of Italy. Jordan glanced at her while she slowly ate and appeared to be content with the lull in conversation. The waitress took their plates, replaced them with clean ones and returned with a basket of hot rolls. A few minutes later their entrees arrived. Their conversation took on a life of its own as they discussed the upcoming photo shoot and the final preparations for the grand opening.

"Thank you for introducing me to Declan. They are beyond perfect in understanding and interpreting how I want Glass Works represented." The more they talked the more excited she became.

Jordan took her hand. "I'm so happy to have had a small part in helping you get closer to your dream."

Callie hadn't let herself fully immerse in believing the dream was becoming real. She took a steadying breath. "I've been waiting for the shoe to drop."

Jordan tipped her head but didn't let go. "Why would you think that would happen?"

As much as Jordan had been an integral part of the process, she had to remain steadfast with her focus on the business now that it was moving from a folding table with handwritten signs and boring displays to a more professional space. She slipped her hand away. She didn't want to confuse her desire for Jordan with her wanting the joy of knowing she'd made it this far. "Because whenever I tried to be proactive about getting my business going in Florida it all went to shit." Callie didn't mean to sound bitter, but when Jordan flinched, it was obvious she'd failed.

"Not that I don't think you could have gotten there sooner than you realize, but I'm glad you chose the city of Rehoboth to plant roots, and once the whole area knows about your work, you might be able to expand if that's something you've considered." Jordan's gaze settled, her face relaxed. "You can achieve everything you desire."

Was that true? Jordan seemed sure she could succeed, but she'd also done the lion's share of the work, so was the accomplishment hers or Jordan's? "If there's not enough demand for my product in the area, I could always teach."

Jordan set her fork down. "But that's not what you want to do, is it?"

Callie slowly shook her head. "The crafts I'm offering for sale, along with the portfolio I've created of the commissioned pieces I've done, are a testament to the art I love creating." Those items, like the items she'd made in the house Jordan had built, were her signature style and how she interpreted her customers' vision in glass. "It's very satisfying to see my work displayed. I think my grandmother felt much the same way about the art she created in the short time she was drawing."

Jordan nodded to the waitress who'd appeared and asked if she was done.

Callie glanced down to find her own plate nearly empty. Where had she been between bites? "You can take mine also."

"Would you like coffee or dessert?" Jordan asked.

She folded her napkin and placed it on the corner of the table. "I'm stuffed like a turkey. It was really good."

Jordan chuckled. "So am I. I'm glad you liked it."

She finished the swallow left in her glass and set it down. When the bill came, she was determined to pay her share, but Jordan wouldn't hear of it.

"I invited you for this celebration. Another time," Jordan said as she placed her card on the bill tray and handed it back to their waitress. Once the bill was paid and they were outside, Jordan's expectant gaze held hers.

"Are you in a hurry to get back?"

The inkling that their time together might end at her door didn't sit well. "No, I'm not."

"Let's go this way." Jordan's hand moved to the small of her back and guided her toward the boardwalk. Little did she know Callie would follow her just about anywhere and the unexpected rush of pleasure confirmed she was falling for Jordan. She was going to have to find out if Jordan felt the same way before her heart told her there'd be no turning back. Maybe it was already too late.

❖

The rhythmic lap of waves against the shoreline's shifting sand steadied Jordan's otherwise racing heart. She and Callie had strolled along the boardwalk for a bit before the urge to be closer to the water drew her toward the beach and Callie had joined her without hesitation. As they strolled, the damp sand was cool against the bottom of her feet. Her mind was a whirlwind of thoughts and desires, each one vying for space and fighting to be heard.

"Where are you?" Callie tugged her hand, their fingers entwined, as they often were when they walked side by side.

Jordan hadn't revealed her thoughts to anyone other than Mel in so many years she wasn't sure she knew how. "Lost in thought, I guess." She tried sounding light, but it came out more solemn than it should have. Callie stepped in front of her, her green eyes reflecting the streetlights from the boardwalk.

"Will you tell me?"

"I haven't had a very good track record with women. I usually fuck it up before it's even begun." She glanced at the ebb and flow of the ocean. It reflected her own tumultuous internal tug of war before she faced Callie again. "I don't want that to happen between us."

Callie stepped closer. "What makes you think it will?" She brought their joined hands to her lips and kissed her knuckles. "History is not destined to repeat itself, unless you let it."

Callie always seemed to have the right answers. Or maybe it was her optimism that made Jordan upbeat about the future because what she wanted more than anything else was turning what may have started casually with Callie into a relationship with substance. Something that mattered to them both. "You said you wanted to enjoy the moment. Not push things."

"That doesn't mean it won't become something more as we spend time together." Callie closed the short distance until their thighs brushed, sending a shiver of excitement through her.

She brushed the windblown curls from Callie's face. "I'll follow your lead then."

"Let's head back and I'll show you how I'm feeling." Callie tightened her grip on her hand and walked backward, giving her a sultry smile.

And just like that, Callie calmed her restless soul with the promise their night wouldn't end on an unfinished note.

CHAPTER TWENTY-TWO

The bright sunlight streaming through the bedroom window let Callie know it was late. She rolled to her side and glanced at the clock. Nine thirty. She rarely slept past eight. She also rarely had a reason to sleep late, and the all-night sex was a great one. She reached across the bed only to find it empty, and a stab of disappointment threatened to spoil the lingering languid feeling of utter physical satisfaction. Callie threw back the covers and was about to get up when her bedroom door opened. Jordan stepped in wearing a sports bra and jeans that weren't zipped while carrying two steaming cups of coffee. Her center tightened, and when Jordan glanced at her naked body, she stilled where she was.

"It's not a good idea to tease me when my hands are already occupied."

She laughed. "I'm not teasing. I thought you'd left, and I was going in search of clothes."

Jordan carefully sat next to her and handed one mug to her. "Are you in a hurry to hide your beautiful body from me?" She brushed her lips over her cheek, the softness of the motion both tender and enticing.

Heat infused her cheeks and she tried to hide it by laughing. "Haven't you seen enough of me for one day?" Visions of orgasms and kisses that took her breath away flashed before her. Jordan moved her warm fingertips over her throat and trailed them down her cleavage.

"I hope I never tire of wanting you." Jordan stiffened, her face taking on a stricken look.

Callie reached for her, grasping her forearm. "Hey, what's wrong?"

Jordan shook her head. "I didn't mean…it sounded like I'm already thinking of the next time. There's no pressure."

Thinking about what Jordan had said on the beach along with just now made her regret giving the impression she wasn't interested in anything more than a casual fuck or two. She didn't make a habit of uncommitted sex, but Jordan had no way of knowing that. The justification of holding that tidbit from her wasn't intentional. To be honest, she hadn't known what to expect when she'd given in to her attraction to Jordan and slept with her. It wouldn't have been the first time she'd found her bed partner incompatible with her daytime desires, and if that happened with Jordan…well, she hadn't wanted Jordan to think if they slept together once she was going to make a habit of it. Of course, that was her rational mind speaking because right this minute her mind wandered to wanting more of the fantastic orgasms Jordan had given her.

Callie had never had anyone who was able to draw her to the edge of climax over and over without making her wish she'd just take her. She enjoyed the constant state of arousal she was in, sometimes for so long, she couldn't breathe. Thing was, it wasn't just the sex. Jordan gave her glimpses of what life with someone who cared about her well-being would look like, regardless of either's social status. She couldn't let Jordan continue to think she wanted less with her instead of more.

"I like that you want more."

Jordan looked hopeful. "You do?"

Callie took Jordan's mug and her own and placed them on the stand, then straddled Jordan's thighs. "I do." She nibbled on her lower lip, licked a trail to her ear, and sucked the tender spot she'd found there that excited Jordan. "In fact," she said as she thumbed Jordan's prominent nipples, "I wouldn't mind doing it again."

Jordan swallowed hard. "Now?"

She pushed on Jordan's shoulders until she was on her back and trapped beneath her. "Right now." After placing a kiss on Jordan's trembling abdomen she sat up. "Unless that's not what you want." She snaked her hand into the vee of Jordan's jeans, making her moan.

"Oh, I want. God…" Jordan said, then gasped. "You make me crazy."

"Mmm." Callie pulled the material up to free Jordan's breasts. "That's good. Right?" She cupped the firm flesh and sucked her nipple into her mouth. Jordan held her hips and pressed upward.

"Yes." Jordan's voice was rough. "Very good."

She'd gotten to touch Jordan through the night, but she hadn't tasted her. "I want these off," she said as she began to tug at Jordan's pant legs. After a few grunts and groans, Jordan was naked. She placed kisses over her lower abdomen, the curve of her hips, her inner thighs. Jordan moaned as she settled between them. Inhaling, she let Jordan's scent fill her. Jordan's swollen clit peeked from her center and Callie couldn't resist pressing the tip of her tongue to the hard knot. Jordan's legs tightened.

"I'm not going to last if you keep doing that."

Callie smiled against the trim hair covering Jordan's mound. "Let's see if I can't keep you right there for a while," she said. "I remember being where you are a few times last night and thought I'd return the favor." When she placed her mouth over her wet slit her desire was to make Jordan squirm and beg for release, but her determination slipped when Jordan's hips rose to meet every swipe of her tongue. Jordan shivered beneath her and when she held her breath and her body went rigid, Callie knew she was going to come. She lifted her head and Jordan opened her eyes. "Now?" Jordan only nodded as though she couldn't find her voice, her hands fisted in the sheets. She slipped her lips around Jordan, alternately sucking and caressing her with her tongue. Jordan's fingers twined in her hair as she pressed upward. With a primal roar, Jordan thrashed beneath her. Callie had never felt so powerful. She slowly released Jordan and placed a light kiss on her still trembling abdomen before moving beside her.

"You wreck me," Jordan said.

She resoundingly kissed Jordan's mouth. "I do what I can." She smiled as she trailed her fingertips over Jordan's bicep, across her ribs to the side of her breast, and she liked how her nipple pebbled in response. Jordan growled then flipped over her.

"If you think you're the only one who wants more, you're wrong." Jordan's hot mouth covered hers.

She had nowhere to be and wasn't about to stop Jordan from doing what she enjoyed, but if they were going to keep having dinner and sex, she wanted to be sure that's what she wanted, too. She had to be sure Jordan was going to be as supportive as she had been during the renovations. Otherwise someone was going to get hurt, and she prayed that wasn't in either of their futures.

❖

The grand opening of "Glass Works" was scheduled for three o'clock the next day and Jordan wanted to be sure everything was perfect though she knew it was all up to Callie. She'd ordered a dozen pink-tipped roses to arrive before noon. The desire to do more rode her hard, but Callie liked her independence and that kept her from acting on her impulses. She made a promise to herself to respect Callie's wishes. The annoying buzz of her phone pressed her into answering without looking at the screen.

"Spade." Whoever was on the other end, she was in no mood for, which wasn't new. Callie was the only one who could change her emotional state from boiling over to a calm simmer.

"Boss, it's Luke. There's a problem on Lansing."

Of course there is. She didn't want to be pulled off one site for issues at another, but that was the name of the game in the construction business. "You don't want to tell me what the problem is?"

"No. But you should come over."

She suppressed the growl rising in her throat. "Fine." She ended the call and headed out to her truck. Jordan took a breath, then another. She didn't want to show up pissed. That was how she used to react when she was frustrated. Before she made a conscious effort to change. It hadn't happened overnight. She told herself life wasn't meant to be lived angry all the time, the way she'd been living since...

As Mel had so eloquently told her more than once, there was more to life than being mad at the world because of the way things turned out. Life could change, and people could help her get to a different place. Not everyone was out to play the blame game or be the first to point the finger, much like Jordan had done to herself. As she pulled up to the jobsite, Luke was standing by the front door looking for all the world like he'd been caught doing something nefarious. She remembered being in the same predicament a time or two. Whatever had happened, she'd fix it. Almost everything could be fixed. Almost.

Jordan got out, met Luke on the walkway, and threw her arm around his shoulder. "Tell me all about the latest crisis and we'll see if we can't figure out a way to rectify it." Luke's surprise was evident in his wide-eyed expression. "I'm not an ogre all the time." She chuckled and turned them toward the door. She was going to need to take a hard look at what she was projecting toward her crew. Her mother often said, "No act of kindness, no matter how small, is ever wasted." It wouldn't hurt to be a little more understanding, and that was a direct result of Callie's countenance. Callie had asked about her relationship with her mother, and she'd been honest about there not really being one. Is that what she really wanted though? To remain estranged and aloof to her mother's grief?

She shook her head. Callie was good for her psyche, and the idea of having her around long term admittedly scared her. She'd confessed she usually fucked good things up, but maybe that had more to do with her own pessimism than reality, and it was time for a change in how she viewed the world...and her own life...if she had any hope of finding peace.

❖

Excitement sent tingling tendrils of anticipation through every fiber of Callie. She'd been waiting for this day for the last six years and now it had finally come. After receiving her teaching degree she'd foolishly listened to her parents and taught middle school art classes while she continued her glass design apprenticeship with a woman she met in one of her college art composition classes. After that, she worked on honing her craft, making pieces for family and friends until one suggested she go into business for herself. That seed had taken root and while the teaching gig provided a means for her to save capital, it was never something she saw herself doing full-time for the rest of her life. She turned in a slow circle to commemorate how far she'd come.

She'd scored a couple of display cases at a fair price from a store whose owner was retiring and selling everything. They held some of the more fragile, smaller items and on top was her binder containing pictures of past works and sample drawings of future pieces. Another held photos she'd collected of all types of stained glass, from suncatchers to window hangings to full length plates.

The vase of roses from Jordan that had been delivered yesterday sat on one of the cases, a constant reminder of her ongoing support of Callie's dream. She tipped her nose to the blooms and inhaled their fragrance, indulging in a moment of peace before the public streamed through the doors. At least, she hoped there were that many visitors.

The refreshment table was stocked with meager pours of champagne, bottles of water, finger foods, and sweets. Callie was confident if customers asked, she could master the details of any pictures brought to her. That's where the real money was. Commissioned pieces weren't just for the rich though, they were for everyone, and she did her best to keep her prices reasonable based on the hours necessary to complete an item along with the materials used. She'd never be rich because of her art, but that was the case for most people in the art world.

True to her word, Declan had delivered brochures, flyers, and her business cards to all the local merchants who sold her items, as well as restaurants and other venues willing to promote a local artist. In total, she'd handed out more than a hundred packets of information. If even a third of that number showed today, she'd count her opening as a great success. While she waited, she tweaked displays and adjusted the lighting that Jordan had insisted be controllable so she could highlight things just right. She smiled at the memory of her and Jordan going back and forth over the necessity of the feature. In the end Jordan had won. It proved to be a valuable addition in the showroom, and she was glad she'd given in to her persistence.

"Ready for your hoard of customers?" Jordan stood in the open doorway looking as hot as the first time she'd set eyes on her.

"I think so." She glanced around for what seemed like the thousandth time.

"Try to remember to breathe," Jordan said, a lopsided smile lifting one side of her face.

Callie laughed. "I'll do my best."

Jordan stepped closer, her gaze dropping for a second before returning. "I know I shouldn't, but I really want to kiss you."

"What makes you think you shouldn't?" She held her breath, praying Jordan wasn't about to tell her there wasn't going to be a next time. That the flowers were a good-bye gesture and thanks, but no thanks. That their business together had come to an end.

"People will be coming soon."

She peeked around Jordan. "I don't see anyone so that can't be a reason."

Jordan pulled her in. "Then no reason not to kiss you." Jordan's mouth covered hers in the softest, most gentle kiss she'd ever had. It was tender and loving and spoke volumes without words. When she pulled back, she moaned at the loss, and her eyes fluttered open.

"That was an amazing kiss, and I want more of them."

"That can be arranged." Jordan's breath lifted the hair from her cheek.

She was about to take her up on the offer when she heard voices approaching. Jordan took a step back.

"Your customers need you. I'm not going anywhere."

Callie's heart fluttered against her ribs. Jordan said the right things at the right time. She was someone she could imagine spending more than just another pleasant night with. She was looking toward the future and a lifetime. She hoped it was the direction Jordan was moving in, too.

CHAPTER TWENTY-THREE

Harry sat on a bench in the small park across from one of the many strip malls in town, his bundles piled around him where he could see them. Jordan hadn't meant to neglect him, but she had. Between work and Callie, days had turned into weeks and guilt washed over her. She ducked into the convenience store, loaded a bag with food that wouldn't quickly spoil and bottles of water, then filled several coffee cups and put them in a carrying tray. Balancing her goods, she made it across the street without dumping anything, amazing herself. Just before she reached him, Harry turned her way.

"Well, well," Harry said. "If it isn't my long-lost friend." He smiled, showing the gap in his teeth, larger than the last time she saw him.

"I know," she said while she studied him for other signs of poor health. Seeing none, she put her bag on the ground and sat next to him. Jordan handed a large paper cup to Harry. "Just the way you like it."

He cocked an eyebrow before taking it. "This a peace offering?"

She winced. Harry wasn't one to beat around the proverbial bush. "Kind of." She peeled the lid off her smaller one and blew across the steaming liquid. No matter the temperature outside she enjoyed coffee, and so did Harry.

"Thank you for this." Harry raised the cup to his lips, blew once, then slurped.

"You're welcome." She pointed to the loaded bag. "That's for you, too." Jordan glanced around. "Where's your cart?" Harry's possessions were usually piled into a grocery cart, going everywhere he went. It was odd that she didn't see it anywhere.

"Damn thief. Some derelict took off with it when I was sleeping." He took another sip. "At least he left my goods. I'd have been pissed as hell and out for blood otherwise."

"When did that happen?"

Harry looked up at the pale blue sky. "Week, maybe two."

"Son of a…" she said, mumbling under her breath.

"Now don't you get all half-cocked. The middle of the night isn't something you could have prevented so stop fussin'. What's done is done."

She should have been around. She knew where to find him and where he slept. Maybe she *could have* done something to prevent another assault on Harry's existence.

"So, where you been?" Harry studied her intensely. His stubble didn't detract from his watchful bright blue eyes.

"Oh, you know, work." She drank the still hot coffee, ignoring the burn as she swallowed. "I've been spending time with Callie, too."

Harry put the lid back on his cup and set it beside his foot, saving some for later like he always did. Jordan had tried to give him a loaded coffee card so he could have some whenever he wanted, but he refused to take it. "That pretty woman I met a month or two ago with the green eyes?"

Laughing, Jordan smiled. "That's the one."

"'Bout time you hooked up with someone nice. She's a looker, that's for sure."

She knew Harry meant no disrespect, and she agreed entirely. "I like her a lot, Harry."

"Mm-hmm. I could tell." He stuck his hand in the bag of goods and rummaged around until he found a sweet roll. "She looked pretty interested in you, too," he said as he unwrapped the pastry.

Jordan hoped what Harry said was true in the long haul. She was terrified she'd say or do something to ruin her connection with Callie. She wasn't about to have that conversation here. "You good?"

Harry waved her on as he took the last bite. "Yeah." He shoved the wrapper into the side pocket of a duffel bag she'd bought him last Christmas. Jordan got up, but Harry's weathered hand stopped her. "You take care of each other, you hear? That's important."

Jordan studied the serious nature of his gaze and the sternness in Harry's voice. She'd never heard him take on a hard tone before. "I will. You take care of you."

He winked at her. "Always do."

She made a mental note to go to the big box store and pay someone for one of their huge carts. Harry wouldn't take money and had refused her offers to bring him home or help him find a shelter, but a cart was his mobile home, and she had an inkling he wouldn't put up too much of a fuss if she brought him one.

Jordan drove to the grocers as she recorded a list of items she wanted to pick up. Callie was coming to her house in two nights when she would make one of her few signature dishes. Her favorite was shrimp scampi, but the idea of breathing garlic all night wasn't something she wanted to do on a date, so she was going with her second favorite creation, chicken and broccoli alfredo with a wedge salad. It would take her most of the day and she'd make a mess, but doing it for Callie would be well worth it. She strolled down the aisles tossing things into the basket and humming some nameless tune. When she realized she was doing it, she stopped where she was. She couldn't remember if she'd ever been so happy about anything in a long time.

❖

By small business standards, Callie's open house had been a huge success. Over forty people had toured the shop and showroom, and she'd gotten more than a dozen orders, including a few specialty and commissioned pieces. Over the last several days she'd finished some of the smaller orders, but she couldn't wait to get started on the huge wall hanging a customer wanted for the entryway of their new forty-two-hundred-square-foot home. Of course, the woman had picked out one of the largest pieces of glass as the central color and it stood behind a number of other sheets of glass, all of which would have to be moved in order for her to free it.

Callie put on her work gloves and began to carefully move glass out of the way. She'd almost reached it when her phone rang. She considered ignoring it, but with her business cards having been distributed, she didn't want to miss the chance of another sale or a new order. She shook off her gloves and picked up her phone.

"Glass Works. This is Callie. How can I help you?"

"Hi. It's Brenda from over at the Sea Turtle Inn."

Brenda had been one of the attendees last week and Callie was pleasantly surprised to hear from her. "Sure. I remember. What can I do for you?" Brenda went on to ask if she could do a series of sea turtle ornaments to sell at the inn. She wanted a total of twenty in five different designs. Before they hung up she promised to get back to her with an estimated cost in the next couple of days, but Brenda didn't seem overly concerned with the details. She said she was glad to promote her work and the inn at the same time. With all the publicity from the open house, she was going to have to start booking jobs out. Maybe she'd need to hire an assistant apprentice soon. What a wonderful thought.

A glance at the clock confirmed she still had about an hour left before she had to start getting ready to go to Jordan's for dinner. Jordan had been so excited when she told Callie she was going to cook for her, and she was looking forward to the meal. The blueberry pie she'd made earlier in the day was sitting on the counter and a pint of hand-packed vanilla ice cream was in the freezer. She had time to move that piece of glass to her big table and plan out some of the pieces. If she was careful, she'd have enough left for some of the background for the turtles. Getting rid of the huge sheet would be good. She'd found it on a random stop at a business in North Carolina during the long drive up from Florida. The owner was liquidating all the contents of a showroom before renovations and this piece had been used as a backdrop for jewelry. It was a little scratched in a few spots, but she decided she could work around those. The price had been too good to pass up.

The behemoth stood almost six feet tall. She should have asked Jordan to help her move it, but she had done so much already, Callie didn't want to take advantage of her generosity. She stood in front of the glass, formulated a way to attack the move, and gripped the edges of the three-foot-wide sheet by first tipping it away from the wall before bending her knees to lift. It was heavier than it looked, but she managed to get it off the floor a few inches. Callie began walking it over toward the table when it began to slip. Her gloves lay where she had tossed them and the edge of the glass pressed against her sweaty palms as she struggled for control, knowing even the slightest bump on the floor could shatter it. Her grip slipped a little more and the rough edge dug into her hands. Two more steps and she was able to lean it against her worktable. Gingerly removing her hands, Callie grimaced at the thin red lines along her palms that were oozing tiny drops of blood. Lucky for her that was the only damage done. She'd had worse cuts when she first started by slicing open a finger on a piece of glass that had required stitches. These, while they burned, looked worse than they were. If she was going to be to Jordan's on time, she had to get moving. She stared at the offensive material and knew she'd press Jordan into service again to get that monster onto the table without breaking it. Had there ever been anyone she could rely on for support when it came to her work, or anything else? The idea of Jordan being that solid post to help hold her up when things got rough lifted her spirit, like it had so many times in recent weeks. She wondered if trusting someone who had a hard time trusting themselves was wise, but when it came to Jordan she found all she could do was trust her own heart.

❖

Jordan swung the door open and drank in every detail of Callie as she stood with the setting sun at her back. Her long, thick hair glistened, the curls more prominent than she could remember at any other time. Her green eyes sparkled with warmth. She wore dark leggings and a magenta three-quarter-sleeve sweater that looked as soft as her alabaster skin. Callie took her breath away. "Hi."

Callie smiled. "Hi. I brought pie." She lifted a foil-covered dish. A bag swung from her wrist.

"Great. Let me take that." She took the dish and when Callie's hands moved away, two large bandages were visible. Jordan quickly set it down and gingerly slid the loops of fabric off her wrist and guided Callie farther inside. "What happened?"

"Me and a sheet of glass had a grudge match."

"Apparently you lost." She studied the bandages, unable to see much beyond a thin, dark line beneath each one. Callie laughed and the sound lent a bit of relief.

"I actually think it was a draw." Callie brushed her fingertip over her cheek. "We both came out of it okay."

She closed her eyes. When she opened them, she pointed to the palm she still held. "This doesn't look okay." Maybe if she'd gone over and checked on Callie instead of doing whatever she could to *not* think about her, or the bed they shared, she could have—

"Jordan, it's all right. I forgot to put my work gloves on, and the rough edge got me. That's all."

Knowing what had happened didn't make her any less anxious. "Okay. I believe you."

Callie moved into her arms. "I will need your help lifting it onto the table if you don't mind."

"You know I don't mind," she said as she wrapped her arms around her and kissed her soft, warm lips. She'd kept herself busy most of the day with cooking and cleaning, more so that she didn't think about Callie and what she hoped they'd both be doing later than because the house needed it. Now that she was here in the flesh, she was done resisting her rising desire, and she wanted to make sure Callie knew it. She slowly pulled away because if she didn't the meal she'd made would never make it to the table. Fueling her body was important if she had anything to say about the night ahead.

"Wow." Callie swayed a bit, then laughed.

"Something funny?"

"No. Everything is great." Callie took a step back. "What smells so good?"

"Chicken and broccoli alfredo." Jordan brought the pie to the kitchen and placed it on the counter.

"There's vanilla ice cream in the bag."

She plucked out the container and slid it in the freezer then pulled a bottle of Sauvignon Blanc out of the fridge and held it up for Callie's approval. When she nodded she cracked the seal and poured into their glasses.

"That sounds as good as it smells." Callie sipped the wine and hummed in apparent delight.

Jordan produced a small charcuterie board, hoping it wouldn't ruin their appetite. She hadn't had much to eat all day and she was ravenous. Callie snagged a wedge of cheese, popped it in her mouth, and moaned.

"Thanks for this," she said and pointed to the display. "I haven't eaten all day and I'm starving."

"Confession." Jordan shoved one hand in her jeans and snagged a tomato with the other. "I haven't either, and I need some stamina."

Eyebrow cocked, Callie looked amused. "Are you going to run a marathon?"

Jordan nibbled on a cracker, her own mouth twitching as she fought a grin. "Not run. I don't want to hurry when I make love to you all night."

Callie studied her, her gaze unwavering. She reached across the counter to touch her hand. The contact was soft, fleeting. Jordan wanted more of those touches.

"Then we should both indulge in sustenance with a hearty appetite." Callie moved her hand away and she was tempted to catch it and bring it to her lips for a tender kiss.

"I'll put the pasta on." She could have stood there looking at Callie forever. Her chest tightened at the admission, and she couldn't help wondering what Callie would think of her desire.

"Can I help?"

Jordan wanted to ask if she could love her with all her flaws and frailties, but that conversation would have to wait until later. The last time she let someone all the way in had nearly destroyed her, but Callie wasn't Shelley and she would keep reminding herself, because whether or not her head was ready, her heart told another story.

CHAPTER TWENTY-FOUR

Callie cut cucumbers and tomatoes for the salad while Jordan set the table and put the finishing touches on the alfredo dish. The aroma of bread baking brought back memories of Sunday dinner at her grandmother's. The one person who never questioned that she would walk her own path, choose her own life to lead, not what her parents wanted her to. She hadn't thought of her grandmother in too long, and she wasn't someone Callie ever wanted to forget. It was why she always wore the tiny cameo necklace her grandmother had given her on her eighteenth birthday.

"Do you want this on the table?"

Jordan turned from the huge bowl she was mixing. "That would be great. Can you fill our glasses, too?"

Callie did as asked, then watched Jordan move about the kitchen and she admired how reaching for something caused the muscles in her back to ripple. She remembered how those muscles flexed as she ran her hands over Jordan's back while she pressed into her, and then she thought about how it would feel if Jordan were to wear a strap-on while fucking her.

"Callie? Is everything okay?" Jordan stood in front of her holding the steaming pasta bowl, concern creasing her forehead. How long had she been daydreaming?

"Yes. I'm fine." Heat suffused her face. She would die of embarrassment if Jordan asked what she'd been thinking. Jordan continued to look her over for a few long beats, then nodded her head before putting the bowl on the table.

"Shall we?" Jordan waited until she was seated before taking her own.

"I can't wait to dig in." Callie busied herself with diving in to her wedge salad as a cover to her pounding heart and the tingling sensations coursing through her. She flicked her eyes at Jordan as she scooped pasta. "Are you planning on inviting the neighborhood?"

Jordan laughed. The sound was magical. "I never learned how to scale down this recipe for a small crowd. You'll have to take some home." Jordan kept scooping. "Damn, I forgot the bread."

"I'll get it." Callie abruptly stood and headed to the kitchen, eager to break the spell Jordan had unwittingly woven around her and sent her imagination careening off in a direction that would only make her more flustered. She took a breath, muttered to herself, then brought the basket to a waiting Jordan. After a few minutes of not looking up, Jordan reached for her hand.

"Are you sure you're okay?"

She set her fork down and finished chewing before meeting Jordan's expectant gaze. "No. Not really." Hard as she fought for control, her libido had been ramped up since she walked in and there was little she could do to tamp it down.

"Is it your hands? Do you need to go to—" Jordan said as she started to get up.

Callie waved her off. "Sit, sit. My hands are fine." Left with no choice, she was determined to keep a cool head. "I've been a bit preoccupied fantasizing about you." There. She'd said it out loud. Jordan's face visibly relaxed, though she continued to hold her hand.

"Tell me about it."

She felt like a fool discussing her sexual fantasy at the dinner table, but the vision remained clear as day. "Jordan, I can't."

"Please?"

Jordan's thumb gently rubbed the fleshy part of her hand, encouraging her to share her thoughts. "I was thinking about you wearing a strap-on and fucking me."

Jordan's eyes darkened. "Is that something you'd like me to do?"

"Yes, but only if you want to."

Jordan slid her hand away and picked up her glass and drained the contents. "Let's finish our meal." Jordan retrieved the wine bottle and poured into each glass until it was empty before sitting again. Jordan's body movements were stiff and there was fire in her eyes.

Her appetite for food was gone. In its place burned a primal hunger for Jordan to take her hard and long and make her scream. Embarrassed by the depth of her need, she avoided Jordan's gaze until she couldn't eat another bite.

"Not hungry?" Jordan asked, her voice rough and deep.

If she was going to let Jordan see what was really going on with her, now was the time. "Not for food," she said as she held Jordan's gaze with her own. Jordan pushed away from the table, stood next to her, then bent down until her lips brushed the shell of her ear.

"I'm going to fuck you until you beg me to stop, then I'm going to fuck you more." Jordan scooped her up in a power move that froze the air in her lungs. "Is that what you want?"

"Yes." She wrapped her arms around Jordan's shoulders as they moved down the hallway. Once inside, Jordan set her on her feet.

"Undress and get ready for me." She disappeared into the bathroom and shut the door, leaving Callie to stand shaking as she fumbled with her clothes, so anxious for the next part she had to sit to get her leggings off. She moved to the center of the bed and tried to pose in a way Jordan would find sexy and wanton, but all she could do was sit and hug her knees in an attempt to calm her frayed nerves. She wanted this, and apparently Jordan did, too. She hoped the lustful gaze would still be there when Jordan joined her in bed.

❖

Jordan placed both hands on the sink and leaned forward, meeting her reflection with resolve. She hadn't been prepared for Callie's confession of wanting to push their sexual forays into another level of play. But damn. It was so fucking hot that Callie could be honest about what she wanted.

She laughed quietly as she pulled off her clothes. She reached in the closet to the top shelf and pulled down the velvet box that hadn't seen the light of day in a few years. Jordan stepped into the straps and made some adjustments. She'd lost weight over the dormant interval. After slipping one of three dildos into place, she grabbed several rubbers and a tube of lube, checking the expiration date of each. Once she was satisfied, she pointed to her reflection.

"Give her what she wants. Take what you need."

The words were familiar even if they sounded a little rusty. It had been her way of psyching herself up to do what she enjoyed. There was a small part of her, one she hadn't let surface for a long time, which liked taking a more active role in what happened in the bedroom. With a critical eye, Jordan evaluated her body. She saw it every day, but rarely looked at herself to appraise what she saw.

In her opinion, her arms were one of her best features. Years of lifting heavy concrete blocks had contributed to helping keep her in shape. What she saw was the best she had to give. If that's what Callie wanted, who was she to question it? She opened the door, the cock bobbing up and down as she moved. Callie was sitting up with her arms wrapped around her knees until Jordan took in all of her. Then Jordan climbed in, kneeling close.

Callie leaned back on her extended arms, moving her eyes to look at the dildo, and her legs fell open. "Oh, yeah," Callie said. "I want to see and feel all of you."

The words gave Jordan an ego boost and she captured Callie's lips for a smoldering kiss. The one she'd been waiting for since

Callie's revelation. When she could no longer breathe, she sat back as she walked her fingertips over Callie's chin, down her throat and leaned in to nip at the tender flesh of the indentation. Not hard, but with enough pressure to let her know she wanted to devour her in every possible way, but not before she knew what motivated Callie's fantasy.

"How long have you been thinking about me this way?" She nuzzled Callie's earlobe.

"When you were working in the garage…" Callie began before she moved the hair from the nape of her neck and placed kisses in a line.

"Tell me more." Jordan moved to the delicate curve of Callie's shoulder.

"Your legs…" Callie moaned. Clearly, she was having trouble focusing. "And your ass would tighten when you climbed the ladder."

"I did that a lot."

"Yeah." Callie exhaled a sigh.

She cupped her breast and blew a warm breath over her nipple, enjoying how it puckered and grew. "And what were you thinking when I climbed?"

Callie squirmed, her eyes fluttered. "I…I can't think."

She stopped touching her and rose on her forearm to read what was written on her face. "Please tell me."

"Power. I saw strength in your movements. I wanted you to focus that power on me with the thrust of your hips."

It was her turn to groan. "I want that, too." She moved over her and slipped her hand between them. Her fingers sank into the copious wet heat and she gathered moisture to coat her dildo, then rubbed her length over Callie's swollen center.

"Jordan?" Callie's voice was strained and wanting.

"I'm right here, love," she said before covering Callie's mouth with hers, then slipped slowly inside. Callie's hips rose to meet her, and they began to move together as though they'd been lovers for decades. Being with Callie felt like home.

❖

Callie hadn't meant to fall asleep. As she looked toward the big bay window the first hints of dawn began to show. Her body was a little stiff when she tried to move but was satisfied in ways she hadn't imagined it could be. She looked at Jordan and studied what she saw. Her face was relaxed, the small crow's feet barely visible. Her chest rose and fell in a steady rhythm. The sheet was tangled around her muscular torso, making her look even more sexy, if that was possible. But what she noticed most was the way her own heart felt as it beat in her chest. For the first time in her life, she knew as she worked toward making her dreams and desires come true, Jordan was the one she wanted by her side if she let her.

No longer able to resist the urge, she rolled onto her side and kissed Jordan's cheek. She watched as she began to stir and refused to feel bad about waking her. When Jordan's eyes opened and she smiled, warmth spread through her. "Hi."

Jordan stretched. "How long have you been awake?"

"A little while." She trailed her fingers over Jordan's shoulder, liking how smooth and firm she felt. Then their eyes met, and Jordan seemed wide awake.

"Callie," Jordan said softly but clearly. "Last night was amazing." She pulled her in and kissed her. The kind of kiss that short-circuited her mind and sparked her body to respond.

When they broke away she saw all the emotions that ran the gamut. The kind she'd dreamt of one day finding in a partner. Gentleness. Kindness. Understanding. Desire. And as soon as Jordan feathered kisses down her neck, the only thought she had was never wanting their time together to end. She leaned in and ravished Jordan's mouth with a hunger she didn't know she possessed.

Jordan gasped for air. "If you keep that up I'm going to want you again."

"You don't want that?" She trailed her fingers over Jordan's abdomen and liked the way she trembled beneath her touch.

Jordan trapped her hand against her stomach, growled, and flipped her to her back. "Are you sure *you* want more?"

"I've never been surer." She ran her hands up Jordan's sides, lightly scoring her flesh and making her squirm. "I want us to be together in every way possible." She meant every word. "Please?" Any hesitation Jordan might have had quickly vanished as she kissed her way across her chest, taking one nipple in her teeth to tease and taunt as she moved her hand lower.

Jordan lifted her head to look deep into Callie's eyes. "I hope you never feel like you have to beg for what you want." She lowered until the length of her body pressed to Callie's and the flame from the kiss that followed set her soul on fire, an inferno that burned red hot, and Jordan knew that Callie was the one she'd been searching for...waiting for. But as much as she wanted to say the words, she couldn't verbalize what her heart was telling her. "I'm going to go slow." She wanted to memorize every inch of Callie. What made her moan, or lift to meet her, or tremble beneath her. The touches that made Callie's back arch while she grasped the bedding in her fists or dug her heels in. Finally, what made her shout and shiver and call Jordan's name.

Callie nipped at her throat, making her groan. "Okay, but not too slow," she said and tapped her chin.

She shifted to one side, cupped Callie's full breast and rubbed her thumb over the stiff peak. She took the other into her mouth and alternately ran her tongue against her nipple. Time passed, and still she coaxed Callie with slow caresses, though she was careful to not stay in one place too long.

After a string of soft oaths, Callie threaded her fingers through her hair and pulled. "Please, please. I need to come." The words came out as a breathless plea.

Jordan was torn. She wanted to be buried inside Callie when she came. At the same time, she wanted to be kissing her. To feel her tighten and still as she tumbled into the abyss. Most of all, she wanted to be there to catch her. And finally, to *be there* when Callie needed her the most. Somehow she found the perfect position to do everything and when Callie shouted in ecstasy, Jordan held her close. "I've got you, baby. You're safe and I've got you." She lost herself in the sensation of Callie and the fears of the past morphed into hope as Callie mumbled incoherently. She smiled and pulled Callie tighter into her arms as they lay in a tangle on their sides. She'd never felt so complete. She'd never been so in love.

CHAPTER TWENTY-FIVE

Callie smiled as she packed the picnic basket she'd bought from a quirky store on the outskirts of town. One that likely didn't get a lot of foot traffic but had a lot of unique items. She and Jordan were going for a ride, and when they found a good spot, they'd have a picnic for two. It was the first chance they had to be together since the night Jordan had given her what she'd asked for. She'd not known how much she craved Jordan taking her with a strap-on until then, and she was looking forward to the next time, whenever that was. But then Jordan had made such sweet love to her, she couldn't help but feel the act was the result of an emotional shift in Jordan.

The idea of a lifetime of possibilities drifted through her mind more than once. Jordan was someone she could see being with long term. It wasn't scary like it had been when she first thought about it, but Jordan needed to be in the same headspace for their relationship to work and they hadn't yet had the kind of discussion she believed was necessary. Not one of any substance anyway. It was time, though, and she'd decided last night after they'd made plans for today that she would bring it up and see where she stood. There was too much work involved with sidestepping what needed to be hashed out. She wasn't necessarily looking forward to talking about the negatives, if there were any, but there wouldn't be any way to know without a frank discussion. Callie glanced at the clock.

Jordan would be picking her up in a little while. In the meantime, she pulled on a sweater and grabbed her datebook, bulging with a stack of her most recent orders. Her travel mug held her favorite ginger and honey tea, and she took everything out to the picnic table Jordan had brought last week as a surprise.

Business had been brisk, and she didn't doubt there'd be more of the same in the coming month or two with the start of the holidays. Whenever she had time, she made turkey and Christmas tree suncatchers and an assortment of ornaments. The special-order items were still going strong, too. She was making good progress and making her dreams come true at the same time. She'd relented to her mother's constant nagging to visit and had invited them to come for a few days over Thanksgiving. She was looking forward to showing them her business and life. Jordan wasn't the only one she was going to have a serious conversation with. Callie planned on telling them in no uncertain terms that their dreams and need for being near the top of societal status wasn't her dream and never was. Maybe they'd even come around to finally accepting she was doing what made her happy versus making her rich.

But today was set aside for fun and Jordan fit the bill. She jotted down project titles, start and finish dates, making a list of supplies and the like until she heard the familiar rumble of Jordan's approaching truck.

Callie met her on the driveway. "Hi."

"Hey. Ready for our adventure?" Jordan kissed her sweetly. The usual heat was missing but the promise of more to come still rang through.

"I am. I just have to get a warmer jacket and the basket." The day was sunny, but now that they were approaching the end of October the wind could be brisk, especially near the water.

"Let me help. I need to use the restroom before we head out."

Callie chuckled. "Let me guess," she said as she pretended to be sizing her up. "It was a three-cup day."

Jordan groaned. "You know me so well."

She stopped just inside the door and pulled Jordan in for a searing kiss. "I like to think so." She slapped her on the ass as Jordan headed for the bathroom, making her laugh. A few minutes later they were settled in the truck and heading for Rehoboth Ave.

"I have to make a quick stop. There's something I need to give Harry."

"No problem. I'd like to see him again. He's very nice." There were homeless in Florida, but they didn't get to hang around the gated communities, one of which her parents lived in. She hadn't had the privilege of getting to know someone who lived on the streets, and meeting Harry had been eye-opening, flipping her preconceived and inherited view of what those less fortunate could offer to a world off its axis.

Jordan nodded. "Someone stole his cart and I managed to find a replacement. I want to make sure he has it so he doesn't have to leave the only possessions he has somewhere while he does whatever he does."

They cruised along the boulevard and then the side streets that Jordan said Harry hung out on. During the fourth pass, Jordan saw him and pulled the truck into a spot across from the tiny park that boasted a playground, restrooms with showers, and benches scattered among the trees. Jordan got out and waved. Harry saw her, and Callie smiled when Harry's eyes lit up as he hustled across the busy street to meet her.

"Jory," Harry said before he glanced at her and tipped his head. "Out with your girl I see."

Jordan's lips pressed into a thin line as she shoved her hands into her jeans. "Something like that. Listen, I managed to find—"

"Hey!" Harry shouted across the thoroughfare to a group of kids that had gathered around his pile of bags. "Get away from there." Harry shouted at the teens who were opening his bags and strewing the contents on the ground.

"Harry, let me take care of them," Jordan said as she lifted the oversized shopping cart from the bed of her truck.

Harry started waving with renewed shouts as he darted out between cars toward the laughing youngsters. He almost made it, but he wasn't paying any attention to traffic and a car was bearing down on him.

"Harry!" Jordan screamed before the screech of brakes was followed by a loud thud and Harry flew through the air.

Callie ran toward the crumpled figure on the pavement. The car pulled off to the side, the woman inside crying and visibly shaken. Jordan knelt next to Harry, talking to him in a hushed tone. She couldn't hear what she was saying, but the sentiment was clear. She pulled out her cell to call 911, praying all the while that it wasn't too late. When she reached them, Jordan was talking in a soft voice.

"Stay with me, Harry. I've got a new cart for you, and I'll help you load it with all your things." Jordan gently rubbed his hand. "Help is on the way. You'll be okay and I'll be there." Tears streamed down Jordan's face, the tracks marring her handsome face. Sirens wailed in the distance.

Callie stood to wave down the approaching emergency vehicles. She glanced at the scene behind her. Blood pooled beneath Harry's head. He hadn't moved and it looked like he wasn't breathing. The EMTs rushed forward, and she guided Jordan out of their way. Jordan's expression was unreadable though she knew that wasn't what was happening inside her.

"My fault," Jordan said. Her voice low and pain filled.

"What are you talking about? It was an accident."

Jordan faced her, anguish evident in her eyes. "I should have checked on him more. If I had, he wouldn't have had to drag his things around and been vulnerable." She looked on as the EMTs continued to work, though there appeared to be no urgency to their movements.

"Kids vandalized his stuff. You would have stopped the person who took his cart, too, but you couldn't be with Harry all the time."

"Harry needed me, and I wasn't there for him." Jordan turned in time to see the EMTs cover Harry's lifeless form with a sheet. "Just like my father, I was too late." An officer slowly walked in their direction.

"Are you his relative?"

Jordan shook her head. "No. A...a friend."

"What's his name?"

"Harry. I don't know his last name. He never told me."

"Address?"

"He's homeless." Jordan pointed across the street to the stuff scattered around the bench Harry had occupied. "Kids did that to his stuff. He was crossing the street to yell at them, and then..."

Callie didn't know what to do or say. Jordan was obviously grief-stricken and she doubted there was anything that would soothe her pain, but she'd try. "Harry didn't see the car. He was focused on getting back to his belongings." She turned to Jordan. "Let's see if we can find his name somewhere in his things."

"We'll check his person for I.D. Thanks for calling it in." He left and went to speak with the driver again, who was hugging herself as she talked with him.

"Do you want to do something with Harry's things?" She didn't think they should be left behind. Harry had been important to Jordan.

"What?" She looked at her glassy-eyed, as though she wasn't really there.

She led Jordan across the street and sat her on the bench. "I'm going to pick up Harry's things." A few of the bags had been torn, making the task more difficult while she searched for anything that might provide his last name. She was looking up and down the street for a store to get something to put it all in when Jordan stood.

"I'll get the cart." Jordan trudged across the street with her shoulders slumped. Callie watched as she stood next to the cart, her head down. She was just about to go to her when Jordan looked her way and carefully crossed the street to where she waited. "I'll see if the shelter will take his stuff. They knew Harry, and..." She shook her head before helping pile the bags in it, then collected the scattered clothes into a neat stack and placed them in the cart, too. She glanced around the park before she started pushing it toward the boardwalk. "Harry had a couple of buddies, though he preferred to spend most of his time alone. Maybe I can find someone who could use them."

Harry's things, while not new, had been cared for and were clean. She had no idea how he managed to do laundry, or take a shower, but he probably knew all the places that would let him use their facilities. At least Callie hoped there were kind-hearted people here. People like Jordan who did what she could, when she could. They hadn't made it far when a frail woman approached Jordan.

"Hey. What are you doing with Harold's things?" The woman pointed to the duffel bag. Her brows were knit, curled fists on her hips.

"You knew Harry?"

"I do." She cocked her head. "What do you mean 'knew'?"

Jordan glanced at her. She nodded, hoping Jordan could talk about the incident that was still so fresh. "Harry was hit by a car." She visibly swallowed. "He didn't make it."

The woman's hands dropped to her sides. "Shit."

"I was going to take his things to the shelter, but if you two were friends, maybe he'd want you to have them."

The woman glanced from the cart to Jordan and back again. She took a step forward, then another. "I'm Ruth." She held her hand out and Jordan took it.

"I'm Jory. Jordan."

"Ah," she said before letting go. "Harold spoke of you regularly. He took a shine to you."

Jordan's eyes welled with unshed tears.

"Ruth," Callie said. "I'm sure Harry would appreciate you taking care of his things." She looked at the overflowing cart. "If you can't use it all, he probably wouldn't mind if you shared it with others." She glanced at Jordan, but she seemed to have retreated into herself. "And if you find any ID in there that could tell us Harry's last name, would you let the police know? Or us." She handed Ruth her business card.

Ruth's features softened. "Sure, sure. I can do that."

Jordan let go of the handle and nodded.

"You two look good together," Ruth said. She gripped the cart and headed down the street the way she came. Callie wondered how people survived without a place to call home or a person who brought the sense of belonging that Jordan brought to her life. On the tail of that thought came the somber one of how Jordan would handle the loss of Harry. She had the feeling she'd soon find out.

CHAPTER TWENTY-SIX

R eady to go?" Callie asked. "There's nothing more we can do here."

Jordan began to walk toward where her truck was parked and took a wide berth around the tow truck that was loading the car with the broken windshield.

Callie wasn't going to suggest they could carry on with their picnic in light of Harry's death. She didn't really know him but mourned his passing for Jordan's sake.

Jordan pulled into her driveway and left the truck running. She retrieved the picnic basket before meeting her on the passenger side. "I'll call you."

"Jordan, come inside. I'll fix us something to drink." The last thing she wanted was for Jordan to be alone when she was hurting.

"I can't." Jordan made eye contact. "Don't you see? I'm not around when someone needs me. I never have been, and I never will be. I wasn't there for my dad, and I wasn't there for Harry. You deserve someone you can rely on and that's not me." She leaned in and kissed her cheek. Nothing that had happened between them up to now had felt so final.

"Please don't go. This wasn't your fault, and neither was your father's death. You aren't responsible for anyone else's decisions. Or for accidents."

Jordan ran her fingertips down her cheek, a touch so gentle she wanted to cry. "It's nice of you to say so, but I know the truth.

I'm good at failing others and I don't want you to be next." She got in the truck and pulled away.

The blank expression on Jordan's face moved her into action. Callie tossed the food from the basket in the fridge before grabbing her keys and phone. The whole time she'd been thinking about the one person who might be able to reach Jordan and talk some sense into her, but she had no way of reaching Mel. She hadn't met her, and she didn't know her last name. There was only one thing to do. She got in her car and headed to the bar that Jordan frequented, hoping she could find a way to contact her. It was the best she could do, and if this didn't work, she'd find another way. There was no way in hell she was giving up on Jordan.

❖

"Hello?"

"Is this Mel?" It had taken her the better part of two hours after Jordan's departure to get Mel's phone number, but she'd finally managed by starting at the bar, asking its patrons, and being pointed to a local restaurant Mel used to work at as a line cook.

"Yeah. Who's this?"

"I'm Callie. Jordan and I have been—"

"Is Jordan okay?" Mel's tone was urgent and laced with concern.

"I'm not sure." She went on to explain, relaying details of what had happened and how Jordan had blamed herself.

"Fuck. This isn't good. Do you know about her father?"

"You mean about blaming herself for his death?"

They talked a few more minutes and came up with a plan. Callie would look for her in all the places they'd gone. Mel would check her house, then visit their usual hangouts. Even if Jordan wasn't there, someone might have seen her. If either of them found her, they'd contact the other.

"Good luck," Callie said. Dread coursed through her. Despondency could lead to a rash decision and Jordan had experienced more than her share of difficult situations. If she believed there was no hope in redeeming herself, she might end up doing something she'd regret. Callie wasn't about to let that happen.

Mel had sent several texts with updates of no success. After more than two hours of driving around searching, Callie couldn't think of any other places to look. There wasn't anything more she could do and went home. Mel tried to reassure her Jordan would show up at some point. She questioned maybe going to Jordan's instead, but Mel had already checked there. If she found Jordan would she be happy to see her or angry for not being given the space she obviously wanted? She had to trust that Jordan would reach out when she was ready. Until then she'd question if she could have done more to comfort Jordan. Was that how Jordan felt about her father, and Harry?

Resigned that Jordan needed time to herself, Callie was left to pace and try not to worry. Jordan was faced with the death of another person she cared about and hadn't been able to save, though she hoped at some point Jordan would see there'd been nothing she could do to prevent either death from happening.

Chapter Twenty-seven

Jordan drove blindly, her vision eclipsed by her grief and the guilt that followed her from the past. Anguished by letting something happen to Harry right in front of her. She should have been around more in the previous weeks when Callie had been her first, and pretty much only, priority. Maybe if she had, Harry wouldn't have had to abandon his possessions from time to time for necessities and worry over them. Too little, too late. It had been the same with her father and not being there when he needed her to keep him safe from himself. Safe from doing something without thinking it through or considering how his actions would destroy her world. The entire family.

She'd tried to do right by Harry, and that was why she'd searched local businesses until she'd found one willing to let her buy a cart. Callie seemed more than happy to be a part of delivering it. She was beautiful, inside and out, and having her there beside her had meant the world to her. She took a shuddering breath. She was in love.

Admitting her feelings and the love that continued to grow between them made her lightheaded. Enjoying the emotions that accompanied those feelings was a new sensation that hadn't happened since her previous relationship, which hadn't been a relationship at all. She shook her head. The toxic feelings from that time tried to rise to the surface and she pushed them away. Nothing would change the past, as much as she wished she could go back in time. But Callie came from her most recent past, and Jordan wasn't willing to dissect the circumstances that had given her the opportunity to meet Callie. Callie was a study in patience and kindness. When Jordan was at her worst, Callie's true nature shone through with understanding and empathy.

Time ticked by as she drove and thought, unaware of her surroundings as she let the flashes of their moments together rise and fall without judgment. Was what Callie said true? Could she finally accept that her father's death wasn't her fault? Sure, she'd been negligent by her absence, but did that really mean she was to blame for his death? Her heart was heavy as she headed home. She doubted anything would make her change her opinion, but it was time she looked for the truth.

She tossed her keys on the stand then sent a text to Callie apologizing for taking off and that she'd see her soon. The response was immediate and the concern apparent even in the text.

Callie: *Are you okay? Do you want company?*

Jordan: *I'm okay. Sad but okay. I'm home. Thanks for asking, but I need some time to process.*

Callie: *All right. Please take care of yourself. I'll be here when you're ready.*

Jordan: *Thanks. I will.*

There were a number of missed calls and texts from Mel, too, explaining that Callie had called her, and she was worried. Jordan sent a quick text to her, too, saying she'd call her soon.

Jordan took a centering breath. She needed answers she wouldn't find by sitting home having an argument with herself. She stared at her phone before pressing the dial button of the one person who might have answers. The phone rang twice before the person she hadn't talked to in too long answered.

"Hello? Jordan?"

Despite rarely contacting her, her mother's voice brought a sense of belonging she hadn't felt in a while. "Hi, Mom. How are you?" Jordan winced at the stilted conversation as though she were talking to a stranger.

"I'm managing."

Jordan had been doing much the same. "Can I see you?"

"Of course you can. You never have to ask, Jordan."

"Is there coffee? I could pick some up."

"Jor, when is there ever not coffee?"

She chuckled. Her mother always had coffee on and was probably the main reason she was such a coffee hound, like her father had been, too. "I'll be there soon."

As she grabbed a package of cookies from the pantry she pushed the anxious feelings away. Her stubbornness had interfered with her relationship with her mother long enough, and she needed to make things right between them while she got answers to the questions that remained if she had any hope of moving forward.

❖

"Jordan." Her mother pulled her into a hug that even at her small stature was bone crushing. It felt good.

"Hi, Mom." She set the cookies on the table then shoved her hands into her pockets, unsure what to do now that she was there. Her mom stared at her for a minute, her features softened. She looked older than Jordan could remember, and she wondered how much the weight of everything that had happened was a contributing factor.

"It's such a nice surprise to see you." Her mom smiled. "Sit down. I'll get the coffee." She turned toward the counter where two mugs sat next to the pot. "Do you still take it the same way?"

"A little cream would be good. I drink too much of the stuff." She tried for a light tone, but the tremble in her voice must have given her away.

"You don't need to be nervous here. I know things have been strained between us, but I'm still your mom and you're still my daughter." Her mother set the cups down and sat across from her.

"I know. That's all on me." She ran her finger around the rim of the mug as steam rose between them. "I'm sorry I missed your birthday."

"Birthdays are overrated at my age." She took her hand. "And nothing's all on you, Jor. I could have reached out, too." She shook her head, released her, and took a sip. "You're stubborn as hell, just like your father and…" Her voice caught. "You sound so much like him." She met her gaze. "It was hard knowing you were so angry with me. You had your reasons, but we never talked about them."

Jordan grasped her mom's shoulder. "I was angry for a lot of reasons, but that's not an excuse for not talking with you, and I had my own demons to blame."

Her mom patted her hand. "Well, you're here now. That's what matters." They were both silent for a minute as they drank. "I imagine after all this time you're here for answers. What do you want to know?"

Once she started, words and questions poured out of her and they talked about her father and how much her mother had suffered from his death, too. How she'd had to deal with losing not only her husband, but her best friend. Jordan told her all about the toxic relationship and her absence before her father's death. It hadn't been easy to confess her shortcomings regarding both her parents, but it was beyond time. Before she ran out of courage, she told her about Harry and the accident. How there were things that Harry said or did that reminded her of her father, especially his bright blue eyes. She didn't cry. There had been too many tears shed over the past and there was no going back, only forward. Callie was waiting there, and it's where she wanted to be.

Jordan brought their cups to the kitchen and placed them in the sink. "I've got to go, Mom."

"I know. Promise it won't be so long before I see you again." Her mother pulled her into another hug.

She wrapped her arms around her. For all the distance between them, Jordan admitted she missed her mother more than she realized. "I promise."

Her mom held her at arm's length and studied her. "You seem different." She tipped her head. "Happier."

"Thanks, Mom." She didn't want Callie's name mixed in with the heart-to-heart that had happened. Callie and her feelings toward her were a topic she wanted to savor for herself, at least for now. "I'll call you next week. Maybe you could come for dinner?" Her mother hadn't been to her home and that too, needed to change.

Jordan sat in her truck. She *was* happier. Even the sorrow of Harry's death couldn't diminish how much her heart was filled with a new kind of love. Before she could move ahead in her own life, she had a few things to take care of.

CHAPTER TWENTY-EIGHT

Jordan sat on the back porch, a glass of bourbon at her side. It was the first alcohol she'd allowed herself since Harry's death five days ago. Five days since she'd talked to her mother. She hadn't been the only one to not see her father's struggles. Her mother had been right there and not been aware of his internal suffering. Had he been able to hide his pain as well as Jordan had been hiding her feelings since Callie had stepped into her life? Did she want to bear the burden of a wrong that could never be righted any longer, no matter how hard she tried?

No. Her father's death was not her fault. He'd made his decision, and as shocking as it had been for those left behind, perhaps he couldn't see his way clear of his demons. A breath of relief whooshed from her. All this time, people had kept trying to convince her, but she couldn't let go, couldn't get past her grief. And Harry…she'd yelled to stop him. It had been an accident. A horrible, unforeseeable accident. Visions of what she could have done differently would replay in her head. She knew herself well enough to accept that. But maybe this time it wouldn't pull her under, pull her away from living her life to the fullest. It was time she talked to one more person and let them know exactly how she felt. Five days without seeing Callie felt like a life sentence. When she finally pulled to the curb and parked, Jordan smiled. She'd asked Callie to meet her at the home she and her crew had built in the spring. The stained-glass insert in the front door was the first thing she saw and reminded her of seeing Callie for the first time. She let the memory wash over her and closed her eyes while the scene replayed in her mind. As it rolled by, the calm energy that Callie's presence brought enveloped her. The pain that gripped her heart loosened.

Flashes of working together on the garage included Callie's thirst to learn about the work Jordan did, and how to proficiently do each task, which had endeared her to Jordan. In turn, Callie had shown her how she created a piece of her art. The necessary steps of how she took a picture of an object or animal and traced out the parts into separate pieces of glass. Then explaining the intricate tracing, cutting, and welding that would produce a strong, lasting project. All the while, Jordan watched her closely, admiring the movement of her hands, the excitement in her voice, the sheer joy on Callie's face as she did what she loved.

What had Jordan done when she'd faced another devastating event? Instead of relying on Callie's strength to help her through, she'd run and avoided facing her fears. "I'm a fool," she said to the empty cab. She needed to be with Callie, craved her quiet presence and surety about the things that scared Jordan the most. She hadn't meant to abandon her, but that's what she'd done, and she had to fix it before it was too late, before Callie decided to be done with her. That wasn't what Jordan wanted…or needed. She needed Callie in her life, and for once she wasn't going to fuck it up like she always did.

❖

When Callie turned down the street, Jordan's truck was parked across from the house where they'd first met. She pulled behind her and tried to imagine why they were there and what Jordan might say. Callie got out on shaky legs before she slid onto the passenger seat of the truck. She didn't say anything when she reached over to take Jordan's hand. When she didn't pull away she took it as a good sign. Silence filled the cab, but strangely, it wasn't uncomfortable.

Jordan took a deep breath. "Thank you for meeting me."

"Were you worried that I wouldn't want to see you?"

Jordan's mouth quirked into a partial smile. "Something like that."

"I've been worried about you." When Jordan didn't answer she pulled her hand closer. "You were so sad, and I didn't want you to be alone."

"Callie, I'm sorry I've disappointed you. I—"

"Don't, Jordan. You don't get to tell me how to feel. You don't need to give me excuses for the past or for things you have no control over. I don't care about any of that. All I care about is you, Jordan. Here and now, and how we weather moments of doubt and hardship together. That's what matters. That we find a way to move forward." She placed Jordan's hand on her chest. "You and me."

Several long minutes later, Jordan brought her hand to her mouth and brushed her lips over the back of it before letting out a long, shuddery sigh. "I definitely have those moments of doubt." She held her gaze.

"I know. Most people do. Just don't shut me out when they happen. Let's face them head on. Okay?"

Jordan released her hand and got out. Callie's heart pounded in her chest. She was unsure what Jordan was going to do. She opened her door and pulled Callie out and into her arms.

"I love you. So much it scares me sometimes."

Callie's heart thudded in her chest as she wrapped her arms around Jordan's neck. "That's okay. Whenever you get scared, I'll chase the fear away by telling you how much I love you, too." She kissed her slowly, purposefully, carefully. "How does that sound?"

"Sounds like something I can definitely live with."

"Good." Callie smiled. "Why are we here?"

"This is where it all began. I never thought the stranger who pissed me off at the same time she drew me in would end up being such an important part of my life." Jordan pulled her closer. "There might have been a time when my state of mind wasn't so good, but now that I have you to help me through, I'm in a much better place." She studied their clasped hands. "I have some healing to do, but at least I can see the way through it all now. I'm tired of using excuses for my behavior. From now on, I promise I'll rationally face them, no matter what." She looked at Callie, her eyes glistening. "Right beside you."

Callie wasn't sure what the future would look like, but she didn't doubt how much Jordan loved her. The thought of not having a future with Jordan in it had spurred her to find Mel and they'd been in touch daily since then. Having a common goal between them had helped them forge an instant friendship and now she understood why Jordan had run.

Maybe Jordan's ghosts had disappeared for good. Together they'd face demons of the past and the promise of tomorrow.

EPILOGUE

Approximately a year later...

Jordan placed the last box in the kitchen of Callie's former home and turned to Mel. "That's the last from my truck."

Mel turned from the new built-in pantry that she'd managed to fit in the narrow space next to the refrigerator. "Thanks." She glanced at the piles around her, a huge smile on her face. "I can't believe how things worked out."

Neither could she. "I know. I still pinch myself." It had been almost a year since she'd told Callie she loved her, and the following months had been filled spending time with Callie, running jobs and hiring more staff, and making decisions about their future, what each wanted to include as they built a life together. One of those decisions had been for Callie to move in with Jordan since her house was bigger and already remodeled. Funny how things worked out. Mel needed to find a place and had saved Callie the decision of selling versus renting. The renovated garage would remain Callie's workshop and studio, and Jordan planned to build a garage for Mel. It all made perfect sense for a lot of reasons. She hugged Mel. "You good here?"

"Better than good." She lightly punched her chest. "You found one hell of a woman with Callie."

"I couldn't agree more." Jordan fished her keys from her pocket. "See you at the festival?

"Absolutely. I'll text you."

Jordan left by the side door and entered the shop area. "Babe, you all set?"

Callie looked up from the tote she'd just set a small box in. "I'm so excited." She put the top on it and locked the handles. "Is Mel coming?"

"She'll join us a little later. I think she wants to putter a bit. She can't believe how everything fell into place." Jordan opened her arms for Callie as she came closer. "Neither can I."

"Mel deserved something she could call her own. As for us," Callie said before she kissed her. "Fate brought us together because it's what we both deserved."

"Mmm…I know." Reluctantly, she let go. "If we keep kissing you know what will happen. Let's get this stuff loaded. You'll lose your place if we don't show up soon."

Jordan took the largest totes to the back seat while Callie brought smaller ones that held packing materials, gift boxes, and tissue. The folding table was in the bed along with a couple of chairs and the pop-up tent. Callie tossed her backpack in and slid onto the seat. "All set?"

"Yes. Do you think it's going to be busy?" Callie asked as she buckled her seat belt.

"It should be. The weather is perfect." Jordan backed out and turned toward the main street where vendors had paid for display space.

"I lucked out by being close to the boardwalk. That should help with sales."

She reached to take Callie's hand as they waited at the light. "Are you nervous about today?" It was the first major event where Callie would have her own booth and she'd been working every spare minute to have enough stock.

"Not nervous really. Excited. It's one of the reasons I chose this location. I'd read about all of the events they have and knew it would be perfect for my art."

"You're going to do great," Jordan said as she pulled up to the space with "Glass Works" taped to a cone. "Let's get the tent up and then you can work on your display while I go find a parking space." They made short work of the tent and opening the table. "Do you want anything to eat or drink?"

Callie frowned. "I should have packed a cooler."

"Hold that thought." Jordan opened the back driver's side door and removed the small cooler she'd tucked under her hoodie. She set it on the ground next to Callie's backpack. "Drinks and snacks. I'll take you for a real meal after the festival."

Callie hugged her. "Have I told you today that I love you?"

She smiled. "A time or too, but I'll never tire of hearing it."

"I love you."

"That's good because I love you, too." They kissed briefly. "Shit. I just remembered I need to check on a delivery. I might be gone a while."

"Do what you need to do. I'll be fine."

"I don't have a doubt you will be." If Callie suspected anything she didn't show it, and Jordan inwardly smiled. She waved good-bye and headed to the airport, hoping her surprise wouldn't fall flat.

❖

Callie was glad to be off her feet for a few minutes. The crowd had grown as the day warmed from the high sixties to unseasonably warm mid-seventies. She glanced at her phone and her forehead creased. Jordan had been gone several hours and she was beginning to worry. It wasn't like her to maintain radio silence, at least not since they'd pledged their love. Another wave of potential customers made her refocus. She trusted Jordan.

Ten minutes later, she turned to find Jordan standing at the back of her tent. "There you are." She needed to touch her and feel the connection she loved so much. "Is everything all right?"

Jordan leaned in for a quick kiss. "It took longer than I thought. Everything is great though."

"That's good." She ran her hands over Jordan's shoulders and down her arms.

"Miss, could you break away from her long enough to help us?"

Callie hadn't realized there was anyone but Jordan and her face heated. "I'm sorry. I didn't…" she said as she turned around.

Her father chuckled. "That's okay, honey."

With her mouth open, she glanced between her parents and Jordan. "How?" She shook her head. "What are you doing here?" She hadn't seen her parents since Thanksgiving, which had been short and somewhat tense, and she took a step toward them as they met her on the side of the display.

Her mother glanced at Jordan. "Jordan asked if we'd like to see how successful you were. Of course, we couldn't pass up a chance to see our daughter shine." She took her by the shoulders, her eyes glistening. "I'm so sorry we…I…didn't take your art seriously."

"On our way here, Jordan showed us some of the work you've done. You're quite talented. You must get that from Viola, because neither of us have an artistic bone in our body." Her dad laughed.

A few people approached the tent. "I've got to tend to customers. Can you come back later?"

Jordan stepped up. "They're staying a few days. I'm grilling tonight. Mom and Mel are going to join us. I hope that's okay."

Callie's heart swelled. "It's perfect. The people we love will all be together for the first time. Thank you for inviting them."

"Go do what you need to. I'm going to walk around with your folks before bringing them back to the house. I'll help you pack up after the festival."

"Have I told you I love you today?"

"Maybe a time or two but you can always tell me again."

She placed her lips next to Jordan's ear. "I love you, Jordan Spade."

Jordan turned and kissed her. "I love you, Callie Burke."

Her life had gone in directions she never could have imagined, and with Jordan by her side she had no doubt there'd be more surprises in the future. The kind of future she was looking forward to sharing with the love of her life.

About the Author

Renee Roman lives in upstate New York with her fur baby, Maisie. She is blessed by close friends and a supportive family. She is passionate about many things including living an adventurous life, exploring her authentic self, and writing lesbian romance and erotica. Her novel *Body Language* was a 2022 GCLS finalist. Her latest works include *Hot Days, Heated Nights* and *Escorted*. You can catch up with Renee on Facebook and Twitter. She'd love to hear from you by emailing her at reneeromanwrites@gmail.com

Books Available from Bold Strokes Books

A Cutting Deceit by Cathy Dunnell. Undercover cop Athena takes a job at Valeria's hair salon to gather evidence to prove her husband's connections to organized crime. What starts as a tentative friendship quickly turns into a dangerous affair. (978-1-63679-208-8)

As Seen on TV! by CF Frizzell. Despite their objections, TV hosts Ronnie Sharp, a laid-back chef; and paranormal investigator Peyton Stanford, have to work together. The public is watching. But joining forces is risky, contemptuous, unnerving, provocative—and ridiculously perfect. (978-1-63679-272-9)

Blood Memory by Sandra Barret. Can vampire Jade Murphy protect her friend from a human stalker and keep her dates with the gorgeous Beth Jenssen without revealing her secrets? (978-1-63679-307-8)

Foolproof by Leigh Hays. For Martine Roberts and Elliot Tillman, friends with benefits isn't a foolproof way to hide from the truth at the heart of an affair. (978-1-63679-184-5)

Glass and Stone by Renee Roman. Jordan must accept that she can't control everything that happens in life, and that includes her wayward heart. (978-1-63679-162-3)

Hard Pressed by Aurora Rey. When rivals Mira Lavigne and Dylan Miller are tapped to co-chair Finger Lakes Cider Week, competition gives way to compromise. But will their sexual chemistry lead to love? (978-1-63679-210-1)

The Laws of Magic by M. Ullrich. Nothing is ever what it seems, especially not in the small town of Bender, Massachusetts, where a witch lives to save lives and avoid love. (978-1-63679-222-4)

The Lonely Hearts Rescue by Morgan Lee Miller, Nell Stark, Missouri Vaun. In this novella collection, a hurricane hits the Gulf Coast, and the animals at the Lonely Hearts Rescue Shelter need love, and so do the humans who adopt them. (978-1-63679-231-6)

The Mage and the Monster by Barbara Ann Wright. Two powerful mages, one committed to magic and one controlled by it, strive to free each other and be together while the countries they serve descend into war. (978-1-63679-190-6)

Truly Wanted by J.J. Hale. Sam must decide if she's willing to risk losing her found family to find her happily ever after. (978-1-63679-333-7)

A Good Chance by Ali Vali. Harry, Desi, and Desi's sister Rachel are so close to getting everything they've ever wanted, but Desi's ex-husband is coming back to get his revenge and rip apart their chance at happiness. (978-1-63679-023-7)

A Perfect Fifth by Jaycie Morrison. Streetwise pianist Zara Keller and Lady Jillian Stansfield couldn't be more different; yet their connection brings a new awareness of who they are and what they truly want in their lives—including each other. (978-1-63679-132-6)

Catching Feelings by Ana Hartnett Reichardt. Andrea Foster expected to catch a lot of pitches from the Alder Lion's star pitcher, Maya, but she didn't expect to catch feelings. (978-1-63679-227-9)

Defiant Hearts by Lee Lynch. In these stories, you'll find your lovers, friends, and lesbians you wish you knew—maybe even yourself. (978-1-63679-237-8)

Love and Duty by Catherine Young. All Princess Roseli wants is to marry her three lovers, but with war looming, she must instead marry Princess Lucia to establish a military alliance between their planets. (978-1-63679-256-9)

Murder at Union Station by David S. Pederson. Private Detective Mason Adler struggles to determine who killed a woman found in a trunk without getting himself killed in the process. (978-1-63679-269-9)

Serendipity by Kris Bryant. Serendipity brings jingle writer Annie Foster and celebrity pop star Bristol Baines together, and their undeniable attraction keeps them close, but will their different paths drive them apart? (978-1-63679-224-8)

The Haunted Heart by Jane Kolven. A ghost, a ring, and a quest to find a missing psychic—it's a spell for love. (978-1-63679-245-3)

The Rules of Forever by Nan Campbell. After reconnecting at their high school reunion, Cara and Lauren agree to embark on a textbook definition friends-with-benefits relationship, but trying to keep it uncomplicated is harder than it seems. (978-1-63679-248-4)

Vision of Virtue by Brey Willows. When virtue and desire come together, be prepared for sparks in this next installment of the Memory's Muses series. (978-1-63679-118-0)

Cherry on Top by Georgia Beers. A chance meeting leaves Cherry and Ellis longing for a different life, but when Ellis's search for truth crashes into Cherry's insta-filter world, do they have any hope at all of a happily ever after? (978-1-63679-158-6)

Love and Other Rare Birds by Angie Williams. Ornithologist Dr. Jamie Martin and park ranger Rowan Fleming are searching the Alaskan wilderness for a bird thought to be extinct and they're about to discover opposites really do attract. (978-1-63679-108-1)

Parallel Paradise by Mayapee Chowdhury. When their love affair is put to the test by the homophobia of their family, community, and culture, Bindi and Rimli will need to fight for a chance at love. (978-1-63679-204-0)

Perfectly Matched by Toni Logan. A beautiful Cupid named Hannah, a runaway arrow, and just seventy-two hours to fix a mishap that could be the best mistake she has ever made. (978-1-63679-120-3)

Royal Exposé by Jenny Frame. When they're grouped together for a class assignment, Poppy's enthusiasm for life and love may just save Casey's soul, but will she ever forgive Casey for using her to expose royal secrets? (978-1-63679-165-4)

Slow Burn by Missouri Vaun. A wounded wildland firefighter from California and a struggling artist find solace and love in a small southern town. (978-1-63679-098-5)

The Artist by Sheri Lewis Wohl. Detective Casey Wilson and reclusive artist Tula Crane are drawn together in a web of passion, intrigue, and art that might just hold the key to stopping a killer. (978-1-63679-150-0)

The Inconvenient Heiress by Jane Walsh. An unlikely heiress and a spinster evade the Marriage Mart only to discover true love together. (978-1-63679-173-9)

A Champion for Tinker Creek by D.C. Robeline. Lyle James has rescued his dad's auto repair business, but when city hall condemns his neighborhood, Lyle learns only trusting will save his life and help him find love. (978-1-63679-213-2)

Closed-Door Policy by Erin Zak. Going back to college is never easy, but Caroline Stevens is prepared to work hard and change her life for the better. What she's not prepared for is Dr. Atlanta Morris, her gorgeous new professor. (978-1-63679-181-4)

Homeworld by Gun Brooke. Headed by Captain Holly Crowe, the spaceship Velocity's crew journeys toward their alien ancestors' homeworld, and what they find is completely unexpected—and they're not safe. (978-1-63679-177-7)

Outland by Kristin Keppler & Allisa Bahney. Danielle Clark and Katelyn Turner can't seem to stay away from one another even as the war for the wastelands tests their loyalty to each other and to their people. (978-1-63679-154-8)

Secret Sanctuary by Nance Sparks. US Deputy Marshal Alex Trenton specializes in protecting those awaiting trial, but when danger threatens the woman she's falling for, Alex is in for the fight of her life. (978-1-63679-148-7)

Stranded Hearts by Kris Bryant, Amanda Radley, Emily Smith. In these novellas from award winning authors, fate intervenes on behalf of love when characters are unexpectedly stuck together. With too much time and an irresistible attraction, anything could happen. (978-1-63679-182-1)

The Last Lavender Sister by Melissa Brayden. Aster Lavender sells her gourmet doughnuts and keeps a low profile; she never plans on the town's temporary veterinarian swooping in and making her feel like anything but a wallflower. (978-1-63679-130-2)

The Probability of Love by Dena Blake. As Blair and Rachel keep ending up in the same place despite the odds, can a one-night stand turn into forever? Or will the bet Blair never intended to make ruin their happily ever after? (978-1-63679-188-3)

Worth a Fortune by Sam Ledel. After placing a want ad for a personal secretary, a New York heiress is surprised when the woman who got away is the one interested in the position. (978-1-63679-175-3)

A Fox in Shadow by Jane Fletcher. Cassie's mission is to add new territory to the Kavillian empire—murder, betrayal, war, and the clash of cultures ensue. (978-1-63679-142-5)

Embracing the Moon by Jeannie Levig. Just as Gwen and Taylor are exploring the new love they've found, the present and past collide, threatening the future they long to share. (978-1-63555-462-5)

Forever Comes in Threes by D. Jackson Leigh. Efficiency expert Perry Chandler's ordered life is upended when she inherits three busy terriers, and the woman she's referred to for help turns out to be her bitter podcast rival, the very sexy Dr. Ming Lee. (978-1-63679-169-2)

Heckin' Lewd: Trans and Nonbinary Erotica by Mx. Nillin Lore. If you want smutty, fearless, gender-diverse erotica written by affirming own-voices folks who get it, then this is the book you've been looking for! (978-1-63679-240-8)

Missed Conception by Joy Argento. Maggie Walsh wants a relationship with Cassidy, the daughter she's only just discovered she has due to an in vitro mix-up. Heat kindles between Maggie and Cassidy's mother in a way neither expects. (978-1-63679-146-3)

Private Equity by Elle Spencer. Cassidy Bennett spends an unexpected evening at a lesbian nightclub with her notoriously reserved and demanding boss, Julia. After seeing a different side of Julia, Cassidy can't seem to shake her desire to know more. (978-1-63679-180-7)

Racing the Dawn by Sandra Barret. After narrowly escaping a house fire, vampire Jade Murphy is unexpectedly intrigued by gorgeous firefighter Beth Jenssen, and her undead existence might just be perking up a bit. (978-1-63679-271-2)

Reclaiming Love by Amanda Radley. Sarah's tiny white lie means somehow convincing Pippa to pretend to be her girlfriend. Only the more time they spend faking it, the more real it feels. (978-1-63679-144-9)

Sol Cycle by Kimberly Cooper Griffin. An encounter in a park brings Ang and Krista together, but when Ang's attempts to help Krista go spectacularly wrong, their passion for each other might not be enough. (978-1-63679-137-1)

Trial and Error by Carsen Taite. Attorney Franco Rossi and Judge Nina Aguilar's reunion is fraught with courtroom conflict, undeniable chemistry, and danger. (978-1-63555-863-0)